Moving On

Deborah Pierson Dill

Moving On

Contact Information: titleadmin@pelicanbookgroup.com

All scripture quotations, unless otherwise indicated, are taken from the Holy Bible, New International Version(R), NIV(R), Copyright 1973, 1978, 1984 by Biblica, Inc.™ Used by permission of Zondervan. All rights reserved worldwide. www.zondervan.com

Cover Art by *Nicola Martinez*

White Rose Publishing, a division of Pelican Ventures, LLC
www.whiterosepublishing.com PO Box 1738 *Aztec, NM * 87410

White Rose Publishing Circle and Rosebud logo is a trademark of Pelican Ventures, LLC

Publishing History
First White Rose Edition, 2011
Print Edition ISBN 978-1-61116-076-5
Electronic Edition ISBN 978-1-61116-077-2
Published in the United States of America

Dedication

To the Lord, who placed the heart's desire within me.
And to the family who consistently
encouraged me to pursue it.

Prologue

Bobby sat on the cold, hard steel bench in the holding cell of the Blithe County jail. He rested his elbows on his knees and pressed his balled fists to his forehead, squeezing his eyes shut against the harsh, fluorescent lights overhead. The officer who processed him asked if he was ready to make his phone call, but he wasn't. Who would he call, anyway? Not Audrey. He needed to think. He needed to sit here until the alcoholic fog lifted a little and he could sort out this mess.

What had just happened? What had he done? He had been arrested on charges of DWI and assault—his first arrest on either count, though certainly not his first offense. He unballed his fists and buried his face in his hands. What happened to all his great intentions to change, to stop drinking, to stop pushing Audrey around? He'd been doing so well these past few weeks. What happened this afternoon?

He released a heavy sigh and leaned back against the cinderblock wall, knowing.

The news of the fire at the Rhodes' house had spread quickly. He heard about it on his lunch hour and had fought the urge to drive out and offer help right then. He wanted Audrey to call him, to need him. He expected her to. He spent the rest of the afternoon compulsively checking voicemail to make sure he

1

hadn't missed her call, getting angrier with each notification of no new messages. She never called. Why would she with Brent there?

By the time his shift at the feed store ended, he'd been so mad he wasn't thinking straight anymore. He drove back to his mother's house and delved into the case of beer in her fridge without giving a single thought to what he was doing. It had been his brother, Tommy, who tossed the match onto the fumes in his soul.

"You just gonna let it go?" Tommy had taunted him. *"You know, I drove by there earlier. It looked like half the town was out there, with Brent Thomason taking charge. You just planning on letting him have her? After all the years you spent with her, are you just gonna sit by and let him take your place?"*

Bobby raised a hand and dragged it across his chin. It hadn't taken much at that point to rile him. The alcohol had done its work, like always.

"God, I'm...." He let the whispered words trail off. *I'm what?*

Worthless?

Useless?

Detestable?

Yes. He was all those things. He had never disputed that fact. And he tried so hard, but he couldn't seem to break free from his old man's way of living. It shouldn't be so hard. He had decided to change, and now it should just be a matter of doing it. So why couldn't he?

Countless times as a kid he'd cried himself to sleep after a beating, vowing that he would not turn into his father. That if he ever had a family, children, he would never lay a finger on them in anger. They would never have a reason to fear or hate him. All he ever aspired to be was the exact opposite of his father. Yet he turned out just like him, and no amount of effort on his part could ever change that.

"God, please...." He pressed his head back against the cold, cinderblock wall and looked heavenward, desperation nearly driving him onto his knees.

He had never been a praying man. He'd never seen the point. There was no way God would ever listen to him or take an interest. Not after all the vile things he'd done. But the simple phrase slipped out before he could lend a thought to it. And now that it was out there he couldn't help feeling a tiny whisper of hope. Maybe something could change. Maybe it wasn't too late.

"Please, God..." He ventured to reach out again. "Help me."

He knew he'd be spending tonight in here, and he'd most likely face an arraignment tomorrow with a court-appointed attorney at his side. But that wasn't what he petitioned God about now. Tomorrow he would plead guilty because he was. Hopefully, the judge would give him a fine or probation, or maybe both. His brother had been through this enough times that he knew what to expect.

But he was guilty of so much more than the charges landing him here tonight. And his heart and soul pled guilty to all of it, crying out now for forgiveness and healing even though it was the last thing he deserved.

1

Lubbock, Texas
$2\frac{1}{2}$ years later

"Boy, it's really comin' down out there." Fully under the safety of Mrs. McDaniel's covered front porch, Meagan Layne set her toddler down and collapsed her umbrella.

Mrs. McDaniel pushed the storm door open and stepped aside. "Well, y'all come on in."

"I'm sorry we're late." Meagan urged her son across the threshold, maneuvering him gently past his sudden fascination with a small hole in one of the planks beneath his feet. "The phone rings, and I just can't not answer it."

Had she known the caller would be Michael somebody-or-other from blah-blah collection agency wanting to work out a payment schedule for the credit cards her ex-husband ran up and then filed for bankruptcy on, she would have had no problem letting it ring. A defeated sigh slipped out before she could stop it. She should have let it ring. No one but debt collectors called her before eight a.m. anyway. But that information wouldn't interest Mrs. McDaniel.

"Oh, it's all right, hon."

Meagan went down on one knee and unbuttoned Jay's little yellow rain slicker. He grinned sweetly as he let the jacket slide down his arms and onto the floor, then he broke out into song.

"A, B, C, D, E, F, G,...R, F, Q, T, T, G, G,...A, C, G,...X, Y, Z."

"Yea! Good singing!" Meagan smiled and broke into applause when he finished.

Thankfully, Mrs. McDaniel followed suit. It was getting harder and harder to work up any enthusiasm for the alphabet song, especially since she'd caught herself humming it in the shower first thing this morning.

"Hon, would you like a hot cup of coffee before you have to go out again?"

Meagan stood, crossing to hang Jay's jacket on the coat rack by the door. She glanced at her watch and shook her head. "Thank you, but I can't. If I leave right this minute I'll get to the salon just in the nick of time for my eight-thirty appointment. I really should get going."

"Meagan..."

Her heart sank at the wary tone of Mrs. McDaniel's voice. If there was one thing life had taught her to do well these last few years it was detect bad news before it surfaced. Not that right now was a great example of keen intuition. Between the strain in Mrs. McDaniel's voice and the look of distress on her face...well, it didn't take any amount of extra sensory perception to know that whatever she was about to say wouldn't be good news.

"Hon, you know how much I love you and little Jay."

Jay wandered over to a large toy box on the other side of the room and removed its contents piece by piece, tossing them out as if looking for something in particular. Her shoulders sagged and a lump rose to her throat. But she tried to smile when she turned back to Mrs. McDaniel.

"Ray and I...we've decided to move back to east Texas."

Meagan almost gasped. "What?" OK, maybe her powers of deduction weren't so great after all. This news was *way* worse than she'd expected.

"Well, you know, that's where we grew up, and both our mothers still live out there, and neither one is in very good health these days. It'll be closer to all the kids and grandkids. Now that we're both retired, it just doesn't make any sense for us to go on living way out here when our whole family lives in east Texas."

Meagan closed her eyes and nodded, though the feeling of being punched right in the gut lingered. "Of course. Yes, of course. It'll be much better for you to live closer to all your folks."

"I'm just so sorry to be leaving you and Jay in a bind. I know things have been hard on you since...well, since..." Mrs. McDaniel let her voice trail off as she shook her head. "But..."

Meagan opened her eyes again, took Mrs. McDaniel's hand and gave it a gentle squeeze, forcing a smile past the rising ache in the back of her throat. "You should live closer to your grandchildren. They need you."

"I'm so sorry, hon."

"Do you know when you'll be leaving?"

Mrs. McDaniel shook her head, her eyes misting over. "Ray drove out to Beaumont yesterday to make some arrangements. We don't know for sure. As soon as possible. Maybe a month or so."

Meagan drew in a deep breath and let it out again,

then glanced at her watch. "I should go. I'm late. Jay, can you come over here and say bye-bye to your Mama?"

"No," came the sing-song-y little reply from the toy box.

Tears stung her eyes. Jay felt so comfortable here. Mrs. McDaniel had kept him since he was three months old. This was like a second home. "OK. Then I'll see you later."

"OK. Bye, Mama."

Jay had learned to sit up, and crawl here. He'd taken his first steps here. All while she'd been at work. How would she ever find somebody else she trusted so completely to care for her son?

Mrs. McDaniel followed her to the front door. "Have a good day, hon."

Meagan choked back a bitter laugh at the customary farewell and waved as she put the umbrella back up and ran for the car.

It took three tries before the engine finally turned over, and she started to the salon. She glanced at her watch as she pulled away from the curb. Her appointment this morning was a regular. He'd been coming to her every month for about a year now, and he'd never shown the slightest trace of irritability or impatience. Of course, she'd never been late. Maybe he'd cut her a little slack. Tears welled and spilled, further blurring her view out the windshield. It'd sure be nice if *somebody* would.

"OK, God. I know you're in control," Meagan whispered, her voice shaky. "I know nothing that's happened lately comes as a surprise to you. But it's managed to catch me a little off guard. I can't take Jay to work with me. And with the debt collectors calling every other day, I've got to have a job."

Maybe she should file for bankruptcy, too. That would get the collectors to stop calling. But why should she have to do that over debts that didn't even belong to her in the first place? She should have known better than to trust Kevin with credit cards that still had her name on them. When she realized divorce was unavoidable, she thought she was being smart in insisting they close all their joint credit accounts. By then it was too late. The damage had been done, the charges amassed. And although Kevin had sworn he'd accept sole responsibility for the accounts in the divorce settlement, he never did.

Meagan tightened her grip on the steering wheel and took a deep breath as the windshield wipers struggled frantically to keep pace with the rain coming down. "Just make it through today. Tomorrow will take care of itself. I can make it through today."

And why couldn't she? She'd made it through yesterday and the day before that, and the week, and the month, and the year before that. God had taken care of her. His grace had been sufficient. Life hadn't been easy, but she'd been content. Another deep breath and she'd about convinced herself that a bright side waited just around the corner up ahead. It had to.

She touched her brake to take the turn. Then her headlights dimmed and went out. So did the radio. She managed to coast into a parking space after the engine died, but there on the sidewalk in front of her stood a two-hour meter. And it was five blocks from the salon, and, of course, the rain would probably continue like this all day.

Why couldn't it just rain here? Just a slow, steady, day-long rain. The kind of soaking that made you want to stay in bed all morning and just sleep. Bobby Kerr leaned forward, displaced and a little disquieted by a deafening clap of thunder that sounded like it was right overhead. He was no stranger to thunderstorms. But West Texas storms were the worst. Nowhere else could the sky go months with not a cloud and then, suddenly, from nowhere, a storm so violent it could frighten a grown man. Not that he was scared.

The hair on his forearms prickled just before a flash of lightning lit the dark morning sky outside. The lights flickered off, then back on, and another crashing peal of thunder drowned out every other noise for a second or two.

Bobby braced his elbows on his knees, and stole a glance at the cover of a magazine. He glanced around the room, really not wanting to pick the thing up. But just under the huge, boldface type promising thinner thighs in thirty days, was a smaller blurb about saving twenty-five dollars or more a week on groceries. Financially speaking, he did all right. But twenty-five dollars was twenty-five dollars.

A quick glance at his watch told him it was nearly eight forty-five. Meagan never kept him waiting. Even when his appointment fell later in the day and she'd had several other customers before him, she was usually ready for him right on time. But this kind of weather could sure slow a person down.

More thunder rattled the plate glass window. Suddenly it didn't seem quite so solid. He was just about to move away from it when he noticed a figure outside hurrying down the sidewalk toward the salon. He rose to open the door as Meagan struggled to get her umbrella collapsed and inside.

"Bobby, I am so sorry I'm late." The apology came out in a breathless rush. Her face was flushed, probably from the chilly, soggy morning air. She briskly rubbed hands together, then pushed damp hair behind her ears and propped the dripping umbrella against a wall.

"Um..." Bobby blinked and forced himself to look away. He'd always thought Meagan was a pretty girl. But today she looked... She looked beautiful. He glanced back at her. "No problem."

Yep. She looked gorgeous. And there was something uncomfortably intimate about seeing her like this–so early in the morning, with her hair damp like she'd just gotten out of the shower. Something compelled him to glance away again as she slipped her raincoat off and hung it on a peg in the wall.

"Well, come right on back. Oooh–" She brushed past him, so close she almost touched him, so close that he could smell her perfume, then she reached for the magazine on the bench. "Twenty-five dollars a week, huh?"

Meagan tossed the magazine back onto the bench and turned to lead him back to her chair.

Bobby cleared his throat as he followed. "Yeah, it probably involves clipping coupons."

Her laugh sounded cynical. "And who really has time for that?"

"I'd just as soon pay twenty-five extra dollars a week."

Meagan's gaze met and held his in the mirror. He knew he should probably look away, but the way she regarded him now...as if she was really seeing him. For the first time in the year he'd been coming to her for a haircut, she didn't just glance at him for the purpose of identification, her gaze didn't automatically and unwaveringly attach itself to his hair. She really saw him. She smiled softly, then turned and quickly shoved her purse and lunch bag into a drawer. When she turned back to face him she held a cape.

"Did you have to walk this morning?" Bobby's voice faltered, and he cleared his throat. Then he climbed into the chair and let her spread the cape and fasten it around his neck.

"Yes. My car died a few blocks down the street." She misted his hair with a spray bottle and then ran a comb through it. "Just the usual this morning?"

Bobby nodded. "Any idea what's wrong with it?"

Again, her laugh sounded cynical and not at all like her. "Probably something very expensive."

She fell silent–also unlike her. He wouldn't call her a talker, necessarily. But she always chatted pleasantly enough to pass the time quickly. Usually she asked about his job, and had a knack for remembering what they'd talked about last time.

He caught a glimpse of her in the mirror as she turned the chair to get a better angle for his cut.

Was she crying?

He shifted a little in the chair as the silence grew more awkward. Should he say something? Maybe he should ask her what was wrong. But why should she tell him what bothered her? She didn't know him very well, and if she did, she'd know better than to confide in him.

No. From what he could tell, she was a pleasant, sweet, normally happy woman. Better for her if he didn't get involved.

Ask her if she's all right.

More than two years had passed since Bobby had become a Christian. This new lifestyle had required strength and discipline he'd never had to employ before. It had been a huge adjustment. But God's prompting had become increasingly familiar, and he knew that's what he felt now. As sure as he was that he shouldn't get involved in this woman's life, he felt the Lord leading him to do so, anyway. He took a deep breath and glanced up at her again.

No trace of tears now. Maybe she'd recovered. Maybe he shouldn't bring it up and upset her all over again. Maybe he'd just imagined the whole thing.

Ask her.

Bobby cleared his throat. "Um. You sure seem quiet today. Everything OK?"

Her glance met his in the mirror for the briefest second before she returned her attention to her work. She nodded and gave him another soft smile. "Yeah. My day just got off to a rough start. You know how it is."

He nodded. Silence engulfed them again.

Only one other customer had braved the weather this morning. An older man sat at a station on the other side of the salon, having a quiet conversation with the woman cutting his hair. Bobby could see them in the mirror. But all he could hear was the snipping sound of the scissors as Meagan worked on him, and then the electric buzz of the trimmer she used for the final touches.

"How's that look?" She handed him the hand mirror and turned the chair so he could get a look from every angle.

"Looks great. And so fast."

She smiled and unsnapped the cape, lifting it away

from him and shaking it out gently. "I thought I'd try to make up a little time since I was late getting here."

"Well, you did good. Thanks." He stood and pulled his wallet from his back jeans pocket. He took out enough cash to cover the cost of the cut plus a good tip, then he folded the money and handed it to her. Her fingers brushed his hand as she took it from him, and without pausing to think about the impulse he closed his hand around hers. "Meagan, is there anything I can do to help?"

Tears welled in her eyes and began to spill freely. She withdrew her hand and turned to reach for a tissue from her station.

"Not unless you can fix cars." She tried to lighten the mood with a little laugh. But the effort was as transparent as the big window in the front of the shop through which he could see the storm clouds. This involved more than a broken down car. But since she brought it up, and if it would help...

"Well, I'm no mechanic." He grinned, seeking and holding her gaze with his own. "But I've been known to fix a few basic problems. I could have a look. If it's simple enough, I might possibly be able to fix it for you."

"No, Bobby." She sounded mortified. "I was just kidding. I couldn't ask you to do that. It's pouring down rain outside, and you're already running late because of me."

"When's your lunch break?" Bobby stuffed his wallet back into his pocket. "If the rain lets up I'd be glad to come by and have a look. If not then, then after work."

"Really?" She smiled. "You'd really have a look at it? 'Cause I think maybe it's just the battery. But if you have jumper cables then maybe we could get it started, and I could go get it taken care of."

Her suddenly lifted spirit gratified him completely, and he returned her smile. "Just tell me when to come back."

"I'm taking lunch at one today."

"Then I'll see you at one."

She beamed. "Thank you so much, Bobby."

He turned to leave and made it as far as the front door before he turned back to glance at her again. He always turned back to have one last look at her before he left. Ordinarily she'd have already brought out the broom and started sweeping up by now. But today she stood next to her chair, still clutching the money he'd pressed into her hand, watching him go. She smiled at him again before he left.

How many years had it been since he'd done something that made a woman happy? He couldn't remember. Maybe he never had.

❧❦

Jumper cables stretched from the engine of Bobby's truck to her car, and Meagan watched from the sidewalk as he tried again to start it. She could see his hand turning the key in the ignition, but the engine made no response. The car was completely dead. Bobby shook his head and got out.

"I don't think it's your battery." His mouth set into a grim line.

"What do you think it is?"

He shrugged. "You'll have to get it looked at by someone who really knows what they're doing. But, from what you described, I'd guess it's the alternator."

14

He held her keys out.

Taking them, she almost winced at his words. "That sounds expensive."

"It'll definitely cost you more than a new battery." He walked around to the front of the car to unfasten the jumper cables. "Wasn't much help, was I?"

"You were, Bobby. It was so good of you to come out here and at least give it a try. Thank you."

"Wish I could have done more. I wish we could have done this at lunch like we'd planned. This time of day everyone's gonna be closing up. It'll be tomorrow before anyone can even look at it." He put down both hoods.

"I guess we can't control the weather." Meagan watched his hands as he rolled the cables up and stuffed them back into their case. His long-sleeved, denim shirt made it difficult for her to tell much about his build, but he seemed lean and strong, like a man who had worked hard at an outdoorsy kind of job all his life. Ranch work, or construction by the look of him, or something like that. Her gaze slid up his arm, across the hard, broad span of his shoulders, then up to his tanned face. He had dark brown hair–a warm, rich shade that many women were willing to pay big bucks to have chemically created on their own heads–with just the faint beginnings of gray at the temples, as well as in his short goatee, which he never let her trim. And his eyes. His eyes were light brown, warm and liquid, like caramel sauce. She'd always been a sucker for brown-eyed boys. How had she missed his?

"You gonna be OK?" When he spoke his voice sounded faint and distant.

Meagan blinked and looked away. "Um, yeah." How could she not have noticed this man before today? Once every month for about a year he'd been sitting in her chair. This same guy. How was it possible that she'd never really seen him until now? "I think I'll just go and call for a tow truck." She took a couple of steps backwards. "Thanks, Bobby. I really appreciate you helping me."

He nodded. "Don't mention it."

She backed up another step or two. "OK. I'll just...um...go make that call now."

He nodded again. "OK."

Meagan turned and headed back to the salon. *Lord, please don't let me trip.* It would probably take direct intervention from God Himself to keep her from stumbling over a bump in the sidewalk or walking straight into some other unsuspecting pedestrian. *Only* an act of God could prevent such an embarrassment right now because every last ounce of self-discipline she possessed was focused on disregarding the urge to turn and look back at him.

అఙ

Meagan hung up the phone and cast a glance out the front window. At least the rain had cleared up and the afternoon had turned pleasant. Warm for February–almost spring like. She gathered her belongings and headed back to her car to await the tow truck.

Bobby was still there, leaning casually against the front bumper of his big, black four by four.

Good grief! How many years had it been since she'd felt that little catch in her chest, like her heart had just missed a beat? Meagan smiled and felt a delicious heat rush to her face. "You didn't have to hang around."

"I thought maybe you'd need a ride home."

"I'd appreciate that, if it's not any trouble." She looked down, and swallowed. "I don't want to keep you from your family."

Meagan glanced back covertly to find him staring off down the street, a slow smile spreading like honey across his features. "I'm not married."

"Oh." *Oh no!* She nodded and glanced down again. He knew she was fishing for information. He was probably accustomed to women chasing after him–*not* that that's what she was doing. Still, she waited, hoping he would volunteer a little more information. Had he ever been married? Did he have kids, like she did? Did he have a girlfriend? Had *he* taken a sudden interest in her today, like she had in him? Or was he just a nice guy, willing to go so far out of his way to help anyone?

Finally, when the silence between them had grown so awkward it embarrassed her, she let out a nervous laugh. Bobby glanced over at her.

"Strange how it's so much easier to make conversation when I have a pair of scissors in my hand."

The corners of his eyes crinkled as he broke into the most amazing smile, and his chuckle seemed to come from deep within his chest. It warmed her all the way to her toes.

"So." She leaned against the hood of her car, trying desperately to convey nonchalance. "Have you always lived here?" What a stupid question. Still, it was something.

Bobby shook his head and shifted his weight against the bumper. "I moved out here...let's see, I guess it'll be a year ago, next month. From a little town called Blithe Settlement. Ever heard of it?"

Meagan shook her head. "No. But I haven't been too many places. Just 'cause *I* haven't heard of it doesn't mean anything."

"Most folks haven't heard of it. It's a little bitty town. You know, the kind where everyone knows your business. I grew up there."

"And you moved here to work at the feed store? Or to get away from everyone who knew your business?"

He nodded and folded his arms across his chest with a grin. "A little of both. And what about you?"

"Born and raised right here in Lubbock."

"Hey, I've been meaning to get on over to New Mexico and see Billy the Kid's grave. You ever been?"

Meagan grinned and narrowed her eyes at the sudden subject change. "Yeah, once or twice. I've got relatives over in Clovis, so my family used to get out that way."

"About how long a drive is it?"

She shrugged. "Oh, I don't know. It's been years since I've been there. Maybe two, three hours."

"Maybe I'll get out there someday." Bobby pushed himself away from his truck when a tow truck turned the corner. "Here's our guy."

His whole demeanor shifted instantly. Like he was relieved that his good deed was nearing completion. She'd probably bored him. And *why* had she made that stupid comment about not wanting to keep him from his family? Why couldn't a nice, decent man like him ever be interested in her? Why did it always have to be bums, and overgrown boys who had no interest in real life responsibilities?

Lord, why not a man like him?

Bobby briefly explained his perception of the problem to the driver as he hooked the car up to his truck, and within minutes the truck and her car were gone.

That's that.

Bobby opened the passenger door for her, and she climbed up into a cab that was neat and orderly. Junk and trash had always littered the cab of Kevin's truck; paper napkins from fast-food restaurants, old junk mail, receipts, aluminum cans, layers of dust. But Bobby's dashboard shone as if it had been detailed just yesterday.

The ride was quiet except for the directions she gave him along the way to Mrs. McDaniel's house.

"It's this one right up here on the right. The one with the red shutters."

"This is your house?" Surprise underscored his words as he pulled up to the curb and stopped.

The folksy wooden sign beside the mailbox identifying the place as Nana's House probably made quite an impression. Meagan grinned and shook her head. "It's where my son's babysitter lives. We live just a couple of blocks further down. Within walking distance."

"I can wait."

"No, Bobby. You've already done too much. Besides Jay loves to be outside, and the weather's nice. We'll get home before dark."

"OK." He nodded. "If you're sure."

"I'm sure. Thank you so much for all your help. In fact your next haircut will be on the house."

He held up one hand and shook his head. "Not necessary."

"I know." She looked down at her knees. "But it's the least I can do. You've gone way out of your way today."

She searched his face for some clue as to what he thought of her. Some sign of encouragement. He just smiled briefly, blandly, then glanced out the windshield. Meagan took a deep breath and pushed her door open. *That's that.*

The sun had not quite set yet, but in the shade of Mrs. McDaniel's house the breeze felt chilly when Meagan stepped out of the truck. She drew her raincoat closer around her, pulled her purse up onto her shoulder, and hurried to the porch where Mrs. McDaniel waited just inside the front door.

She turned back and waved at Bobby, and then watched his truck retreat down the street after he pulled away. He so obviously wasn't interested in her. And the last thing she probably needed right now was a man further complicating her life. But disappointment swelled at the thought that she wouldn't see him again for another month.

2

Hard to believe a month had passed since the last time he saw Meagan. Bobby pushed fingers through thick hair and glanced at the phone on his desk. It hadn't been for a lack of wanting to. More than a couple of times he'd found himself sitting here in his office, not concentrating, and itching to call her. Just like now. But his thoughts would always turn to Audrey. And those thoughts would always turn into an overwhelming desire to call *her* and ask how she was, to tell her all about his new life, and how he liked his job, and how good God had been to him. How he hadn't taken a drink in two and a half years now. How he really *was* changing this time.

He opened his top desk drawer and pulled out an old photograph of them together. Five years ago today, on his thirtieth birthday, she'd planned a surprise party for him. Just before he blew the candles on his cake out, someone had snapped this picture and then given it to them later. He ran his thumb over her likeness. That had been a good day.

Audrey had probably thrown out all her old photos of them together. He wished he had a few more than just this one. His chair squeaked as he leaned back to study the photo.

All his life he'd only had one good thing, and that had been Audrey. If only he'd taken it upon himself to make certain changes a long time ago, he might not have squandered his opportunity for a happy life with her.

My timing is perfect.

Bobby nodded and whispered, "I know, Lord. I know."

Part of him felt silly for holding onto this old picture–for holding onto that part of his past. Audrey was married now, and happy. Expecting a baby from what he'd heard. But he would always love her. He would always wish that he had been the kind of man she needed.

He slid the photo back where it now seemed to belong–the back of his top desk drawer–and his thoughts drifted back to Meagan Layne.

Last time he saw her she'd needed help. OK, so maybe he hadn't really helped all that much, but he'd tried, and she'd seemed so appreciative. Nervous, too. Bobby smiled. Like a woman with a crush. And for a few minutes he thought he might ask her out. For just a moment he thought maybe he really could start over from scratch, with a sweet woman who knew nothing about him and had no expectations one way or the other.

But she had a kid.

As changed a man as he knew he was now, he couldn't deny the anger and violence that resided deep within him. Maybe he could expose another woman to the possible danger of his temper. He could admit up front what he'd done, and what he might very well do again someday. *God forbid it.* Then she could decide for herself if loving him was a risk worth taking. But he couldn't do that to a kid. He *wouldn't* do it. Not ever.

Besides which, she could be married for all he

knew. He just assumed she was single based upon her reaction to him–her apparent interest, her nerves. But maybe she just felt out of her element, or uncomfortable at spending any amount of time alone with a man when she had a husband. But if she had a husband, why didn't she just call him about her car trouble?

He shook his head. Regardless, in his loneliness, he'd probably just misinterpreted every little thing that happened that day.

A light knock sounded on his halfway open office door.

"Bobby, I'm fixing to take off. Did you get next week's schedule done?"

"Yeah." Bobby picked through the few papers on his desk and pulled one out, handing it to the young man standing in the doorway. "Here. Could you hang it up on the board on your way out?"

"Sure." The kid stepped across the small room and took the page. "See you Monday."

"Have a good one, Rich."

Bobby's gaze drifted back to the phone as Rich's retreating footsteps echoed through the hall and faded to silence. A month had passed since the last time he'd seen her. Whether she was interested in him or not, he was due for a trim. The store was quiet now. But soon folks would begin coming in on their way home from work to pick up what they needed for the weekend. He probably ought to call Meagan for an appointment now, before it got busy and he missed his chance.

Todd, his assistant manager would be here until closing, so he could leave early if she could work him in this afternoon. It *was* his birthday.

∂◦◦ᵲ

Meagan hung up the phone and took a deep breath, trying to calm her suddenly racing heart. She grinned. He needed a haircut. Bobby was on his way right now. Usually he called a couple of days ahead, but today he specifically asked if she could fit him in before closing time. Even if she had back to back customers until dark, she'd have found a way to squeeze him in.

For a month, every time the bell on the front door jingled she'd catch her breath and look up, hoping, despite the fact that it had never happened before, he'd walk in without an appointment. Every time the phone rang she had to restrain herself from dropping whatever she was doing to run and answer it before someone else did.

How lucky that she didn't have another customer today and for the last thirty minutes had sat posted behind the front counter waiting for a walk-in, examining her birthday manicure, and enjoying a piece of the cake the girls had sprung for. Or maybe luck had nothing to do with it. Maybe God was giving her a sign, or a birthday present.

Meagan took a last bite of cake, wiped her mouth, and dumped the paper plate into the trash can under the counter. Trying hard to affect total nonchalance, she stood and walked back to her station to check her reflection in the mirror. Quickly she ran a brush through her hair and put on a little lip gloss.

"So, who's coming to see you?" Alicia, a big-haired Texas girl, had occupied the station next to Meagan's for years. She now stood, brushing color into a young woman's roots, and casting sly glances at

Meagan over her bifocals and between brush strokes.

"What?" Meagan dropped the tube of lip gloss back into her purse.

"Oh now, don't be coy. Not every customer of yours rates shiny brushed hair and fresh lip gloss."

Heat rushed to Meagan's face. She smiled and turned away. "I just had a piece of cake. I needed more lip gloss."

"You're blushing!"

It was mortifying, but true. Meagan looked back up into the mirror to see the flaming pink blush that lit her features.

"Maybe it's a hot flash!" came the response from another station behind her. "She *is* thirty."

"That's no hot flash, that's a *man* flash!" Alicia broke into a cackle, and the other women within earshot followed suit. Even the woman in Alicia's chair, whom Meagan had never seen before, started to giggle. "Come on, tell us. Who is he?"

Their excitement got the better of her and she, too, began to laugh, pressing her cool palms to her hot cheeks. "Y'all stop!"

"Oh, seriously now, hon." Alicia paused to catch her breath. "It's about time you moved on. I mean, you knew that husband of yours wasn't coming back when he served you with divorce papers, right?"

Meagan felt her smile fade, and she looked down. Of all the rotten things Kevin had done in leaving her, having her served right here at the salon had been the most humiliating. Of course, in this setting, sympathy had abounded. All the girls hugged her and talked about what a jerk Kevin was. Alicia, recovering from a rough divorce, had sat right down and cried with her.

Meagan cast a glance back at Alicia, who

continued to exchange teasing remarks about the situation with the others. She was right. It *was* about time she got on with her life. No reason in the world existed to prevent her from finding a good, stable man—one who would love her and Jay. Maybe she could even get married again before Jay got too much older. Having someone would make life so much more satisfying.

Lord, could it be possible?

Silence fell suddenly all around her, and Alicia turned back to her client's head, focusing with unnatural intensity on her work. Meagan turned to see what the distraction was.

Bobby stood, like an answer to her silent prayer, on the other side of the front counter, drumming his fingers and waiting for someone to notice him.

"Oh, I see," Alicia said under her breath. "You go, girl."

Meagan smiled warmly at Bobby and motioned for him to come back to her station. "Just the usual today? Or could I tempt you with a shampoo?"

Bobby reached up and ran a hand through his hair. "What the heck. Sure."

Meagan blinked. In the year he'd been coming to her, he'd never wanted anything but a basic quick cut. Nothing fancy. No shampoo. She'd tried repeatedly to convince him that it cost the same either way, and he might as well get his money's worth, but it didn't seem to matter. "Well, all right," she said at last, turning to lead him to the sinks. "You can just um...have a seat right there." She pointed to a chair while she reached into the cabinet up above for a towel. To her complete dismay, her hands began to tremble as she spread the towel across his shoulders and tucked it into his collar.

She balled them into tight fists when she'd finished, then she flexed them, listening as her knuckles cracked lightly.

Washing hair went with the job. She took a deep breath and pressed her eyes closed for a second. She washed several heads a day. Every day. She could do it with her eyes closed and one arm tied behind her back–so to speak, carrying on a conversation with her client while mentally reciting her grocery list. It was no big deal. And yet right now she couldn't remember the very last thing she'd said. The only thing she knew right now, was that the muscles in his shoulder tensed under her light touch as she guided him back against the chair. He shifted his position until his neck was comfortably cradled in the sink. Then he took a deep breath and let it out slowly.

"So." Meagan ran the water over her own hand until it felt warm, then she ran it over his scalp, working it in with her fingertips. His eyelids drifted shut. "Do you have a big weekend planned?"

"No. No plans."

"Well, it's not every day you come in asking for a shampoo. I was just wondering what the occasion was."

Bobby grinned and opened his eyes. "Oh, I don't know. It's the end of the day. I've been workin' hard in the warehouse. It's my birthday."

Meagan laughed. "Really? Today?"

He looked up at her as she turned off the water and reached for the shampoo. He nodded and closed his eyes again as she began to work the shampoo into his hair. "Is that funny?"

"Actually it is. My birthday is tomorrow."

Her touch, as she gently massaged his scalp with

her fingertips, had clearly begun to relax him. His eyebrows shot up at her comment, but he didn't open his eyes. "Well, happy birthday to you."

"Same to you." She watched his face as she worked, watched as the lines around his eyes and mouth softened, as the muscles in his neck relaxed. Meagan slowed her pace and took a couple of extra minutes to finish–as long as she dared in a salon full of curious women. Then, when she could justify shampooing no longer and she felt in imminent danger of her client falling asleep in the sink, she turned the water back on to rinse.

He stirred and took a deep breath. "Are you married, Meagan?"

She smiled. "Why? Are you about to propose?"

He opened one eye and peered up at her, then he smiled that amazing smile and began to chuckle.

"Because it wouldn't be the first time a man proposed to me while his head was in my sink." She turned off the water and grabbed another towel for his hair. "But, to answer your question; no, I'm divorced."

"I was just curious," he mumbled as she turned and led him back to her station.

He sat, and they settled into a comfortable silence as she worked. Every so often Meagan would look into the mirror to find him studying her. Once she glanced over at Alicia, who winked and grinned. Meagan stifled her own grin for fear that Bobby might notice, and realize how she felt about him.

At last she handed him the mirror. "So, what do you think?"

He looked himself over and nodded. "Looks great. Thanks." Then he reached for his wallet.

"Oh no you don't." Meagan raised one hand to

stop him. "This one's on me. Remember? For all your help last time."

"No. I couldn't ask you to–"

"You didn't. Besides, it's your birthday. Wait! Wait right there." She spun around and hurried to the lounge in the back, quickly cutting a generous piece of her birthday cake and serving it up on a little paper plate, covering it with plastic wrap. Then she hurried back.

"Here." She offered it to him. "I know you probably have friends who will do a lot more. But happy birthday."

"And I thought I wasn't going to have any cake today." His wide, soft smile almost took her breath away. "Thanks, Meagan. I guess I'll see you next time."

She nodded, smiling despite the disappointment that made her throat ache. "Bye." Her voice sounded just a bit tremulous. "Have a good weekend."

Meagan turned and reached for the broom as he walked away. OK. So he didn't ask for her phone number. She swept up quickly. Maybe she should have offered it. Or asked for his. Would that have been too bold? It couldn't have been any bolder than the little scalp massage she'd just given him. She squeezed her eyes shut and stifled a groan. How embarrassing!

God, what was I thinking?

A little stash of folded money sticking out from underneath a hair spray can caught her eye when she put the broom aside and turned to reorganize her combs and scissors. She grabbed it, unfolded it and counted it. Then she spun around to see Bobby in his parked truck, just outside the large front window. He gave her a grin and a little wave, then he looked over his shoulder and backed out of his parking space.

Meagan turned to Alicia, who was having a quiet conversation with the girl in her chair, a timer on the counter next to her ticking off the minutes left for her color.

"Did you see him do this?" Meagan held up the cash.

Alicia nodded. "Oh, yeah."

"And you let him? I wasn't gonna charge him today."

Alicia shrugged. "Who am I to butt into a lovers' quarrel?"

Meagan sighed and glanced back at the now empty space where he'd been parked. He'd waited there until she spotted the money. Then he'd smiled and waved and driven off, without asking for her number. And now it would be *another* month until she saw him again.

ॐॐ

Bobby didn't make it five blocks down the street before some irresistible force made him take the next right hand turn and begin circling back around to the shop. He didn't know much about stalkers, but he hoped he wasn't turning into one. He knew what kind of man he was. Plenty of times he'd shown up someplace unwelcome and ended up causing trouble. Maybe he should turn the truck back around and head on home.

He turned right again.

He sat back against his seat and took a deep breath, remembering the feel of her fingers in his hair as she washed it. He couldn't remember the last time someone had touched him beyond a handshake or a friendly pat on the shoulder at work or at church. Her touch had been like a salve to his heart, and she'd realized it, too. He knew how long it took to wash his hair and she had taken three or four times that long.

He made another right hand turn.

Surely it wouldn't hurt to ask for her number. Just to call her every now and then. Just to have someone to talk to, possibly someone to have a nice dinner with. He wouldn't ask more of her. She was young and pretty. She'd want to find a good, stable, reliable man. Maybe get married again. He'd never make good husband material, and definitely not good father material. Or would he?

"Lord, could it be possible?" he asked softly, as he slowed to make the right turn that would take him back to the salon.

He parked on the opposite side of the street and turned around in his seat to watch for her. Her car was still parked in front, but, from where he sat, it didn't look like too much business was going on. The lights inside went out. They were closing up. He'd just run across the street when she came out and ask for her number, and if he could call her sometime. Nothing more.

A wry chuckle escaped him, sounding oddly loud in the silent interior of his truck. There was a time when he didn't give a situation like this so much thought. If he saw a pretty woman, and he wanted her phone number, he'd just walk right up and tell her so. That's how he met Audrey. He'd seen her around town, and heard about how she was nursing a broken heart. When he spotted her alone at the diner one afternoon he'd just invited himself to her table and made it a date. Simple.

So why had his hands gone cold and his mouth dry?

He looked back over at the salon when a group of laughing women came out. One locked the door behind them. But Meagan wasn't among them. Maybe she'd had car trouble again and had needed to make other arrangements to get home. He should have asked.

He squinted and strained to detect some movement inside the salon that might indicate whether or not she was still there. But he saw nothing. He sighed and ran a hand across the back of his neck. Then he saw her, about a block further down the street. She walked back toward her car holding hands with a dark haired little boy who couldn't have been more than three.

You stupid, good for nothin' son of a–!

The words rang through the recesses of his memory, pushing their way forward until he wanted to raise his arms to shield his head and body from the blows that always followed.

Can't you do nothin' right? Can't even put the lid on the garbage can to keep the dogs out of it. How many times do I have to tell you? What are you, retarded? Or just plain stupid?

The exact infraction never seemed to make a difference. And it never seemed to matter if, whatever it was, was a first time offense by a seven-year-old kid who honestly didn't know any better. The punishment was always the same and yet never consistently applied. One day, leaving his bike out in the front yard might rate a rib cracking beating. The next, no one seemed to care. Before supper the television was too loud, afterwards not loud enough.

His mind reeled forward about twenty years, to the life he'd shared with Audrey. All she'd asked him to do was turn the television down so she could talk on the phone. He remembered hearing every derisive, profane word that his father had ever uttered coming out of his own mouth that afternoon. And then he had punched her.

Bobby balled his right hand into a fist and pressed it into the palm of his other hand. He had punched her—not slapped, or shoved, but punched her—right in the face. He spread his fingers flat in front of him, then he covered his eyes and tried to rub out the vision of her terror stricken face and bloody mouth, of her small form huddled in a protective ball against the wall while his attack continued, of coming to his senses, vaguely realizing through an alcoholic fog what he was doing and what he had become. And then later that night, finding out she'd been pregnant as she lost the baby...

He dropped his hands onto his lap and looked back over at Meagan who had stopped by her car and knelt down to tie her little boy's shoe. The child stood right in front of her, both his hands on her shoulders, grinning down at his mother's manipulation of his shoe laces. When she finished, she looked up and said something which prompted him to throw his arms around her neck and kiss her.

The only thing Bobby had ever aspired to be when he grew up was the exact opposite of his father. But he'd managed to turn out just like him.

"God, what am I doing here? What was I thinking?"

Of all the things he'd never have, missing out on a family of his own grieved him most. He didn't have it in him to be that kind of man. Meagan thought he did, though. He could see it in the way she'd looked at him this afternoon. She thought he was good, or at least better than her ex-husband. Who must be a total moron to have had a woman like that and let her go. He shook his head as he watched her buckle her son into his car seat, then get into the car and drive away.

The less she knew of him, the better.

3

This was probably the stupidest thing she'd ever done.

Meagan stopped abruptly in the middle of the parking lot as a stiff gust of wind kicked up a dust devil in the vacant lot to her left. What business did she have at a feed store? She lived in a forty-year-old subdivision with zoning restrictions prohibiting the grazing of livestock. She didn't even have a dog. Or a cat. So what excuse would she give if she actually happened to run into Bobby while she browsed the shelves?

She didn't have a clue what sort of stuff they sold in feed stores—aside from feed. She'd never set foot inside one before. Such a complete city girl was she that the only cows she'd ever seen had been from her car window as she drove down the highway. Horses made her completely nervous. She wouldn't even touch one when she had the opportunity for fear that it might bite her, or kick her, or step on her.

Another gust caught several strands of her hair and freed them from the clip which held the rest captive. Meagan half turned to go back to her car. If he'd been interested he would have done something about it. He would have asked for her phone number, or taken it upon himself to look it up, or called her at the salon. She wasn't hard to find. So the only logical conclusion here was that he didn't have the slightest interest, and she'd make a complete fool of herself by going into this store and nosing around nonchalantly where she obviously had no business.

But he had asked her if she was married. That had to mean something. If he didn't care to know, he wouldn't have asked, right? She turned back to the store front. Plenty of attractive men crossed her path in the normal course of her day. But none since Kevin had so totally attracted her.

She could do this.

She would go inside and look for him. And if she didn't see him, she would ask for him. If he wasn't interested he could just say so, straight out. She'd feel like a total idiot, but at least she'd know for sure.

With a deep breath and slight nod, she gathered her courage and pressed forward. The automatic door slid open and she stepped across the threshold, pulling off her sunglasses and shoving them into her purse.

She looked up, and her already pounding heart stepped up its pace. Bobby stood about twenty yards directly down the middle aisle. He had his back to her as he talked with a customer. But there was no mistaking him. She veered quickly to her right.

God, what am I doing here?

This had been such a stupid idea, and now it was too late to back out. The minute she made a break for the door, he'd probably turn around and see her fleeing. Then what would he think?

Frantically she looked around.

Pet carriers! She was surrounded by all makes, models and sizes of pet carriers. She didn't need one. But she might…if she got a kitten. She'd always kind of wanted a cat. It would probably be good for Jay to have a pet to grow up with, too.

Meagan grinned and had to suppress a chuckle. She'd never given half a thought to getting a cat until right now, when the need for a carrier suddenly presented itself.

A picture of a cute kitten graced the carton of one, and Meagan reached for the display model and opened the little door to look inside.

"Is there something I can help you with, ma'am?"

Meagan started and heat flooded her face at the warm almost mocking tone of Bobby's voice. Even with her back to him she could tell he knew what she was up to.

"Do you need a new carrier for your cat? Because we have a good selection, and I'd be happy to show them to you."

She pressed her cool palm to her hot cheek and turned to smile at him. "Do all your customers get such prompt and personal attention?"

Bobby shook his head. "Just the pretty ones."

She blushed again. How could he say such a thing and not be interested? The thought gave her fresh confidence.

He stepped a little closer. "So what kind of cat do you have?"

"I..." She bit her bottom lip and looked down. It really shouldn't be possible at this point, but her face actually grew hotter. "I don't have a cat."

"Really." He sounded as if he had expected no less.

"I'm thinking about getting one."

"I see. Well, let me show you what we have." He launched into an animated spiel regarding all the different pet carriers they had in stock, from the top of the line to the cheap but perfectly functional.

"Bobby." She interrupted just as he was beginning to rattle off his list of all the different styles and brands he could order should none of these suit her.

He turned and raised his brows.

"I, um...I didn't come here to buy a cat carrier."

"No?"

She shook her head. "No."

He propped one arm up on the shelf beside him and leaned against it as that amazing smile spread slowly across his face. "Then what did you come here for?"

She swallowed and pulled her purse up higher on her shoulder, hooking her thumb under the strap and shifting her weight uncomfortably. "I...I don't want you to think that I'm...that I'm..." She took a deep breath and blew it out.

"That you're...?"

She cleared her throat. "That I'm, um, too aggressive. Because I'm not. It's just that..."

He tilted his head to one side, his smile widening.

"It's just that when you came in for your haircut last week, I really thought that..." She let her voice trail off as a sales clerk walked passed them. When she continued, she lowered her volume a little and stepped a bit closer. "I had hoped that you might..." She stalled. Was she really about to do this? She glanced up into his eyes. It was probably all he could do to keep from laughing out loud at her. She clamped her mouth shut and looked away.

What was she doing?!

This was undoubtedly the stupidest thing she'd ever done. He knew exactly what she was trying to say, and he had no intention of making it any easier.

He fully intended to stand there so cool and casual, and watch her flap and jerk and lay her feelings right out in front of him. She definitely wished she'd seen this side of him earlier.

"Meagan, are you trying to ask me out?"

She sighed and looked down. "Would you think of me as a total idiot if I were?"

His warm chuckle drew her gaze back to his face. "No."

"So you wouldn't be against, say, having pizza with me and my son, Jay, sometime? Or we could get hamburgers if you'd rather."

His smile faded.

Meagan's heart stopped. She held her breath as a new wave of heat rushed to her face. Maybe she shouldn't have mentioned Jay. Maybe he didn't want an entanglement that involved another man's child. How could she back out of this now without completely humiliating herself?

"Of course, if you don't want to, it's OK. I just thought that Jay loves pizza, and I love pizza, and if you like pizza, too, it might be fun to get together..." She ended with a shrug and looked down at the floor beneath her feet wishing it would open up so she could dive in.

His silence prompted her to glance tentatively back up. His smile had returned, though it didn't seem quite as wanton as before.

He took a breath as if to speak, but then stopped. He tried again. "Meagan, I..." A long silence followed after his voice trailed off and he studied her face carefully.

He wasn't interested.

Her chest constricted and a lump rose to her

throat. Rejection was the chance she took in coming today. She'd known it before she'd parked outside. But knowing that it might happen didn't ease the sting.

She took a deep breath and gave him her best smile, trying to look charming and sheepish at the same time. "You don't want to."

"Meagan, it's not that—"

She held up a hand and shook her head. "You don't have to explain. It's OK. I understand." She smiled again and turned halfway to leave, then she stopped. "I guess I'll see you next time you need a haircut?"

His smile had completely vanished, and his mouth set into a grim line as he nodded.

"OK, then." The words came out as a tremulous whisper.

That's that.

She turned, wanting to bolt from the building and run to her car. Instead, she kept her pace normal and her head up. Allowing him to know how hard this had been and how much his rejection hurt would only intensify the embarrassment.

ॐॐ

Torn between going after her and letting her go, Bobby expelled a long, heavy sigh as he watched Meagan walk away. She had misinterpreted his hesitancy to accept her invitation. The moment he realized she was trying to ask him out, his heart jumped in some strange combination of admiration for her determination, and regret that she was the one doing the asking.

Just outside the front door she stopped and began

digging through her purse. He took a few steps forward and waited, thinking maybe she'd changed her mind about running off. Maybe she intended to come back in and give him her number, anyway. Maybe he should go out there and put her mind at ease, telling her that it wasn't that he didn't want to take her out, but that he already knew she deserved a much better man. A surge of disappointment gripped his heart when she pulled her sunglasses out of her purse and continued on her way.

He took a few more steps and stopped at the checkout counter, watching her make her way to her car. Her stride was graceful, probably because she was so leggy, and tall—almost as tall as he was.

A gust of wind caught her skirt and twirled and twisted it around her legs. It tossed loose strands of her long, straight brown hair around, and she tucked them behind her ears just before she reached for the handle of the car door.

"You just gonna let her go?"

Bobby started and turned to find Todd standing behind him, stance wide, arms akimbo, also watching her leave. Todd grinned.

He turned back to see Meagan's car pulling out of the parking lot. A deep breath did little to tamp down the disappointment swelling in his chest. He ran a hand across his chin and put on his best back-to-work expression. "It's for the best."

❧

"So what does he look like?"

Meagan grinned drily and shrugged at her sister. "What difference does it make? He's not interested."

"Aw, come on. Humor me."

With a raised brow and an indulgent smile, Meagan took a seat adjacent to Caroline at the kitchen table. She took a breath to speak but stopped short when Jay came squealing by them pushing a big, yellow dump truck as fast as he could.

"Don't you run that truck into any walls or furniture!"

"OK, Mama!" came the reply from another room.

"So?" Caroline prompted.

"I don't know. He's average height, average build. Dark hair, brownish eyes."

Caroline's mouth twisted. "Doesn't sound too heart stopping."

Meagan smiled, but said no more.

"Oh, I see. You plan on keeping him all to yourself."

"I would if he was mine to keep. I'm telling you he isn't interested."

"And what makes you so sure?"

She studied Caroline's wide grin for a moment, then smiled sheepishly and looked down into her glass of iced tea. "I asked him out and he declined my offer."

"You what?"

Jay came running by again, this time without the dump truck.

"Did I hear you right? You asked him out? And he turned you down?"

Meagan nodded. "Yes. So you see, it doesn't matter what he looks like, or if he's a nice guy, or what he does for a living. Because he's not interested."

"When did all this take place?"

She shrugged. "Friday on my lunch hour."

"Wow." Caroline sat back and studied Meagan

with open admiration. "I'm impressed. I mean, that sounds like something I'd do. But not you. Not *my* big sister."

"Well, trust me. It won't happen again."

"Oh, now, you can't win them all. When you fall off a horse you just need to pick yourself up, dust yourself off, and get right back up on it."

Meagan felt a slow grin spread across her face. "What do you know about horses?"

"It's a figure of speech," Caroline said with a sassy toss of her head.

"What do you know about figures of speech?"

Meagan caught Caroline's mocking grin, which accompanied a single lifted brow in imitation of her own skeptical expression.

"So, what's that no good ex-husband of yours up to these days?" Caroline rose from her seat and crossed the kitchen to refill her iced tea glass.

"Filing for bankruptcy, apparently."

"Yeah, Mom was telling me about that. Now the debt collectors are on your back. What are you going to do?"

Meagan shrugged. "I don't know. I've been talking to this one who said he'd be willing to take half of what Kevin owes, and he'd bet that the others would as well. I'm thinking about just trying to pay them."

"What?"

"The only other thing I can do is file bankruptcy myself, and I don't want to do that. What else can I do, Caroline? They call me morning, noon, and night. Apparently, the law is not on my side in this."

As if to illustrate her point, the phone rang.

"You gonna get that?" Caroline asked, returning to her seat.

She shook her head. "Let the machine get it."

"You sure? What if it's your man? What's his name again?"

"Very funny."

"Don't you want to at least turn the volume up and find out?"

"Trust me. It's a bill collector."

"Isn't there at least some kind of law against them calling on Sunday?"

Meagan burst out laughing. "Like it would matter." She turned in her chair to catch a glimpse of Jay in their small living room, stacking blocks one on top of the other, then gleefully knocking them down. "Not so hard, please, Jay. OK?"

"OK, Mama."

He barely touched the block on the very top of his current stack, knocking just that one off. He turned and grinned at her.

"Good boy."

A shower of blocks on the living room floor was the reply.

"So, where is old Kevin calling home these days?"

"Santa Fe, last I heard."

"Santa Fe? No wonder he's out of money." Caroline's facetiously disdainful tone brought a fresh smile to Meagan's lips. "What's he doing in Santa Fe? Besides going bankrupt."

"Trying to find himself."

Caroline shook her head, her gaze drifting to the small child in the next room. "Didn't he look around here before he left?"

Meagan felt her smile fade and she turned back toward Jay, just in time to see him send another tower scattering around the room. "In fact, he did."

The phone rang again.

"See what I mean?" Meagan looked pointedly at her sister and grinned, then she rose from her chair and turned toward Jay. "Who's ready for a bath?"

"Me! Me! Me!" Jay began jumping in place.

"I'm going to give him a bath and put him to bed. Did you get all your stuff out of your car earlier?"

"Yeah, I'm all ready for a week of rest and relaxation."

Meagan scooped Jay up into her arms and carried him to the bathroom. Fifteen minutes later she was drying him off when Caroline poked her head in the door.

"What did you say your new boyfriend's name was again?"

"I didn't, and he's not my boyfriend."

"Are you sure?" Caroline grinned like she was up to something. "Because some guy just pulled up out front in a big black pickup truck, and I think he means to come to the door. I figure it's either him or a debt collector."

The doorbell rang.

"Yep, that would be him."

"What!?" Meagan's heart skipped, then began to pound.

"So, what's his name? You know, so if it's not him I can tell him to get lost."

"Bobby. Bobby Kerr."

"OK. I'll go check him out. Don't be too long."

"Wait!"

Caroline turned back to face her as the doorbell rang again.

"How do I look?"

"You might want to run a brush through your

hair. But otherwise you look perfect. Like a regular girl who's spending an evening at home and not expecting company."

"OK, Jay." Meagan said as her sister disappeared down the hall. "Let's get your jammies on."

She tried not to rush reading his story, or saying his prayers. But the only thing she could concentrate on was the fact that Bobby was here for some strange reason, talking to Caroline–totally unpredictable and outspoken Caroline.

After hugs and kisses, and assurances that his nightlight was in proper working order, she slipped out of Jay's room. The soft murmur of voices drifted down the hall from the living room, and she strained to make out a few words. With a furrowed brow she ducked back into Jay's bathroom to check her appearance.

Caroline had been right. She did need to run a brush through her hair. But all her things were in her own bathroom on the other side of the house. Caroline's brush lay on the counter, however, so she used it. There was nothing else she could do. The water spots all over her faded jeans and light blue t-shirt from Jay's antics in the tub would just have to dry on their own. She wiggled her pink pedicure, wishing she had shoes on, or at least socks. She sighed and gave her shirt a tug. It didn't change anything, but at least she felt like she'd tried.

Bobby practically jumped up out of his seat when she entered the room. "Hi! I...um..." Caroline gave her a covert thumbs up, but had to cover it quickly when Bobby turned back toward her. "Your sister let me in."

Meagan smiled. "Did she offer you some tea?"

Caroline grinned and clamped a hand over her

mouth in mock shame, then she rose and hurried to the kitchen.

"I...I didn't realize your sister lived with you."

Meagan shook her head. "She doesn't. She's visiting for spring break. Please, sit down."

Bobby did so, and accepted the glass of tea Caroline offered with a nod and a smile.

"I guess they don't teach manners in college," Caroline said apologetically.

Meagan grinned. "That's UT for you."

"Oh, you go to UT?" Bobby turned back to Caroline who nodded.

"Yes. But don't bring it up too much in front of Meagan. She went to Tech, and can't for the life of her figure out why I would choose a superior school. Speaking of which, I have an assignment I should get started on."

"Don't mind Caroline. She's the embarrassment of the family. She's an English major. Painfully shy. Always has her nose in a book."

Caroline smiled and wrinkled her nose at Meagan. "Bobby, it was a pleasure to meet you. Now, if the two of you will excuse me, I'll go to my room."

Bobby watched her go, then turned back to Meagan with a broad, disbelieving grin. "You went to Tech?"

She tried, but failed, to stifle a giggle.

His grin widened and softened in response.

"So what am I doing cutting hair? Right?"

He stammered a little. "No...I wasn't gonna–"

"It's OK." She softened her voice to let him know that it really was OK. "I've seen that look a hundred times on the faces of my own parents. They wonder why they spent all that money sending me to college when my cosmetology license was really all I needed."

He swirled his glass around then took a sip. "So, if you don't mind my asking, why did they?"

A smile crept across her features and she shrugged. "I don't know. You'll have to ask them. I tried to tell them when I finished beauty school that I'd found my niche. But they insisted. And I wasn't silly enough to pass up the chance for a college education. Just in case."

He nodded and set his glass on a coaster on the end table, then leaned forward. "I hope you don't mind me just dropping by like this. I looked your address up in the phonebook. I tried to call, but all I got was the answering machine. I thought if I–"

"I don't mind."

He smiled and nodded, relaxing a little. "I was wondering if your invitation for pizza was still open. Because, well, I kind of like pizza, and there's a Chuck E. Cheese's just a few blocks from where you work. I thought your boy might like that."

"You mean, you'd go to a kid's pizza place on a first date just to please my son?"

He nodded and looked down at the carpet beneath his feet. "If it'll make up for my behavior on Friday." He glanced back up at her. "I'm sorry if I hurt your feelings."

Hot tears rushed to her eyes, but she blinked them back. She would *not* cry right here in front of him. Especially not over something she'd already chalked up to experience.

"I didn't mean to," he added quickly. "When you left, I thought about going after you. Believe me, there's nothing I want to do less than hurt your feelings, Meagan."

"It's OK." She took a breath and gave him her most confident smile. "I forgive you."

"Good. Because I'm sorry."

"I know."

"OK." He nodded and rubbed his hands together. "So, you'll let me take you and...and..."

"Jay."

"Jay. You'll let me take you and Jay out for pizza?"

"As sweet an offer as it is, Bobby, I can't subject you to Chuck E. Cheese's with a two year old. Not on a first date. But Caroline is here for the whole week, and I can leave Jay with her for a few hours, so we can go somewhere more grown up."

His smile was totally relaxed now. "I'd like that. If it's not too much trouble for Caroline."

Meagan nodded thoughtfully. "Well, it was the topic of heated debate when we were kids, but we finally came to the conclusion that I *am* the boss of her, and she has to do what I say."

He chuckled warmly and rose to his feet. "OK, then. Um, what night this week is good for you?"

She shrugged and stood, too. "Thursday?"

He nodded, and turned toward the front door. "Thursday. Can I pick you up at six?"

"Yes." Disappointment swelled at his apparent hurry to go now that he was here. "Are you sure you can't stay for another glass of tea?"

"No. I should get going." He met her gaze for a moment, then turned again. "I'll be looking forward to Thursday."

"Bobby?" She laid a hand on his arm when they reached the front door. "Earlier you said you almost came after me on Friday. Why didn't you?"

His gaze lingered on her hand where it touched

his arm, and she drew it back slowly. He took a couple of deep breaths and almost started to speak, then he stopped and swallowed. "I'm a coward. Plain and simple." He smiled and uttered a nervous laugh, then turned and pulled the front door open. "I'll see you Thursday."

She smiled back. "I'll be here waiting."

A street lamp on the corner lit up the evening sky as well as the path down her front walk. She folded her arms against the chilly night air and stepped out onto the welcome mat as goose bumps broke out all over her arms. Bobby waved as he got into his truck, then he started the engine and drove away.

Meagan rubbed her arms briskly and looked toward heaven. A smile bubbled up within her. She may not know exactly who he was just yet, but she was pretty sure he wasn't a coward.

4

"OK. How do I look?" Meagan swept into the room and spun around, putting on her most confident smile despite the butterflies flapping violently in her midsection and the general impression that she was about to have a heart attack.

Caroline looked up from the floor where she and Jay lay coloring together. Meagan turned again for her sister's inspection, and smoothed the skirt of her dress.

"Is that a new outfit?"

"No." She looked down at the smooth turquoise fabric which was sprinkled liberally with dainty pink and white flowers. For a full twenty minutes she'd stood in her small walk-in closet trying to decide whether she should wear a skirt, or a dress, or jeans. She had no idea what type of dress would be most appropriate for a first date with, quite possibly, the most attractive man she'd ever met. But she didn't want to look merely appropriate. She wanted to look beautiful. "Should I have bought a new one?"

Caroline shook her head. "No. It just doesn't look familiar."

"Is it OK? It's not too dressy, is it? I thought a shirtdress would be good, because it's casual but still a dress. Should I go put on something else? Do you think he'll come wearing jeans, I could go–"

Caroline's sudden burst of laughter cut off

Meagan's rambling. "Snap out of it!" She said, getting up off the floor. "I think he probably will wear jeans. This *is* Lubbock. But even so, this dress is perfect. Very feminine. Shows enough leg to intrigue, but not too short." She circled around Meagan, checking every angle. "Your hair looks good, too. He'll like it up. What man in his right mind wouldn't, with that neck of yours?"

Meagan raised her hands to her throat. "It doesn't look too long does it? That's all I need is to look like a huge goose-necked nerd."

"Are you kidding? I've always wanted your neck, and your legs, and your face. Let's face it. You're the pretty one."

Meagan almost snorted. "Oh, please." She raised a hand to the clip in her hair then drew it back again, clasping both hands together in an effort to still their trembling.

Caroline rolled her eyes. "Why are you so nervous?"

"That's an easy question for you to ask, college girl." She smiled at her sister. "You probably have a date every weekend. But the last person *I* went on a date with was Kevin. And that was eight years ago."

Caroline dropped back down on the floor next to Jay and picked up a crayon. "Let me be the first to congratulate you on your improved taste. I never did like Kevin all that much."

"You couldn't have told me that eight years ago?" She glanced at her watch. Bobby would be here in about five minutes. "It might have saved me a lot of grief."

"I don't know." Caroline's tone sounded skeptical. "You really think you would've listened to me? Your little sister?"

Meagan glanced at her sister, who now colored the big nose of a clown in Jay's coloring book. Eight years ago no one could have convinced her that Kevin wasn't her soul mate. Least of all her sister. She sighed. "No. I wouldn't have listened. But you'll never convince me that *that's* the reason you never said anything. I know you too well. And it's never stopped you before."

"You were so happy. I didn't want to spoil it for you." Caroline stopped coloring and covered Jay's ears with her hands. "Kevin was kind of wimpy," she whispered.

Far from being interested in their conversation, Jay shoved his aunt's hands away and scowled at her. He resumed drawing bold purple lines all over her clown.

"Bobby's more of a man. You know what I mean? He seems like the kind of man who can take care of things. Not to mention the fact that he's much better looking." Caroline paused and cast Meagan a sideways glance which was accompanied by an appreciative grin. "I do believe he qualifies as 'hot.' For an older guy."

"He can't be more than–"

"Older than me, not you."

Meagan heard the tease in her sister's voice and she grinned. "He is 'hot,' isn't he?" A nervous giggle escaped, but died quickly at the sound of a car door slamming outside. Her heart began to pound and heat rushed to her face. *He's here! Lord, why am I so terrified?* She took a deep shaky breath and smoothed her skirt. "So, I look OK? I need to brush my teeth." She scrambled back to her room, barely noting Caroline's hollered advice from the living room.

"You might put on a different pair of earrings, too.

Maybe something with a little more dangle. And a little choker if you have one. To show off your neck."

ﾟ⬩⬩⬩

Twice Bobby had raised his hand to ring the doorbell and pulled it back again. He shifted his weight from one foot to the other and rubbed the back of his neck. Never had he been this nervous about a date before. Of course this was the first date he could remember where he hadn't started out with some amount of alcohol coursing through his veins–encouraging him.

The difference tonight wasn't the absence of alcohol, however. He took a deep breath and blew it out. The difference was that he shouldn't even be here.

He turned around, hooking his thumbs through his belt loops, and looked back at his pickup. It would be easy to leave. It'd be no problem at all to just head back to his truck, get in, drive away, and pretend he'd never stood here on Meagan's front porch intending to take her to dinner and start a relationship that would probably end up exposing her and her little boy to his dangerous temper.

It would hurt her feelings. He made a half turn, trying to decide whether to stay or go. But better to hurt her feelings now, than to break her heart, or worse, later. He glanced down at the ground and shook his head. He should go. It was the last thing he wanted to do right now. But it was the right thing. Yet his feet stayed rooted to the spot.

How was it possible that, for more than two years, he'd fought the seemingly ever-present urge to take a drink, and yet now he couldn't summon enough discipline to simply walk away?

Lord, why do I want this so much?

He stood, as if waiting for an answer, or a sign as to what he should do now. But all he could hear was the wind rustling the limbs of newly budding trees. The desolate sound was sign enough, and he turned to go.

The front door opened behind him, and he turned back to find Caroline standing in the doorway.

"Were you planning on ringing the bell sometime tonight?"

Bobby stammered. "I...uh, well, I...I just..."

She grinned and opened the door wide. "Come on in."

"Thanks." He stepped across the threshold into the softly lit living room, noticing how heavy his boots sounded on the wood floor.

"I don't believe you got to meet Jay when you were here Sunday."

At the sound of his name, a little brown haired, blue eyed boy looked up from a large braided rug that covered most of the floor in the center of the room.

"Can you say 'hi', Jay?" Caroline prompted.

The kid smiled brilliantly. "Hi!" He then returned his full attention to his crayons.

"Hi." Bobby grinned.

"I coloring a picture." Jay pointed to a page in his coloring book.

"I see." Bobby dropped down onto one knee beside Jay to get a better look. "What's that a picture of?"

"Elephant." Jay rolled his eyes as if he were tired of the question.

"Never seen a purple elephant before."

Caroline chuckled. "Well, where've *you* been?"

Bobby cast her a quick, amused glance. Then turned his attention back to Jay, trying to determine a resemblance between him and Meagan beyond their shared hair and eye color. He barely heard Caroline when she said she'd go and tell Meagan that he'd arrived. But when he heard two sets of footsteps approaching, he pushed back up to his feet and turned toward them, wishing he had a hat or some other little thing to occupy his hands.

The sight of her nearly took his breath away. He swallowed and cleared his throat. "Hi." He cringed inwardly at the unsure tone of his own voice.

"Hi." Her shy response completely melted his heart. When she ventured a tentative glance at him, he captured her gaze with his.

"You look real pretty, Meagan."

It must have been the blue of her dress that accentuated her baby blue eyes and made them sparkle. Likewise, the soft lamp light was probably responsible for the glossy golden look of her brown hair as it swept up and away from her delicate ears and graceful neck. She was so pretty, and sweet. What right did he have to be here?

She smiled. "Thank you. Did you meet Jay?"

Bobby blinked. *Come on man, pull yourself together. There's no need to stare at her like you've never seen a woman before.* "Yeah." He turned and looked back at the boy who still sat on the floor at his feet. "Yeah. He was just showing me his purple elephant."

She smiled and knelt down next to her small son, pausing to admire his artwork before softly explaining that she was going to leave for a little while, and that he had to obey his aunt while she was gone.

Again, the feeling that he shouldn't ever set foot inside this house began pressing in from all sides. This was her home, the one place in this world where she should be able to expect safety for herself and her little boy. Now he stood in the middle of her sanctuary–a man like him–waiting to escort her out, and all the while she would trust him, not knowing how wary and suspicious she ought to be.

God, I shouldn't be here. Why have You brought me here? What can I possibly give this woman besides a life of fear and pain?

He swallowed and felt the muscles in his jaw begin to twitch as an image of Audrey with a black eye and swollen lip suddenly imposed itself over the cozy picture he now intruded on. Then Meagan stood and turned to face him, smiling radiantly, her big blue eyes taking him in, her expression telling him she trusted him, and she knew he had something to offer.

"I think I'm ready."

He cleared his throat and nodded. "OK then. How does Mexican food sound?"

"Ooh! I love Mexican food!" She reached for a sweater that was draped over the back of a chair and started to put it on. Quickly he caught it and held it open for her, taking extra care not to touch her.

He didn't think his heart could bear even the most innocent touch.

෴

"This is so nice, Bobby." Meagan spread her napkin across her lap and leaned forward in her chair. "I've never been here before. And I can't remember the last time I got to sit down at a nice restaurant, without a baby to take care of, and just enjoy a meal and the company of another grown up. Usually it's just McDonald's for me."

He chuckled warmly and spread his own napkin across one of his knees. "Well, I'm glad I could be here for you. For the record, though, usually it's just McDonald's for me, too."

"Then I'm glad we could be here for each other." She reached for a tortilla chip and studied him covertly as she nibbled on it.

Maybe it was just her imagination, but he seemed uncomfortable. Standing in the middle of her living room he'd told her how pretty she looked. He'd meant it, too. For a minute there he hadn't been able to take his eyes off her. But since, he seemed reluctant to look at her again. He'd barely said five words to her on the drive over here. And even now as he reached for a chip he didn't seem the least bit inclined to talk, at least not without her prompting him. Maybe he was just nervous. That had to be it. *Please, Lord, let that be all there is to it.* Because if it wasn't, this date was not off to a good start.

"So, tell me a little more about this hometown of yours." She flung the suggestion out desperately. It wasn't exactly the makings of sparkling conversation, but it might lead somewhere. And if he wasn't going to call her for a second date, she intended to do everything in her power to make sure it wasn't because he was bored. "I know it's small. And I know people are always into everyone else's business."

His answering grin looked sincere to her, and warm. That was a good sign.

"Then you already know just about everything."

"Come on, tell me about it. Do you have family

there still?"

He sipped his tea and nodded. "Yes. My whole family still lives there. My mother and father, two sisters and one brother. Various aunts, uncles and cousins..."

"So you were the first to strike out on your own. And you came to Lubbock for...?"

"A job."

"The same job you have now? At the feed store?"

He selected another chip from the basket and scooped up some salsa. "The very same. Selling feed and supplies, and um...pet carriers." He grinned and took a bite of his chip.

Warmth flooded her face and she looked down into her glass. "You must think I'm a total idiot."

"No," he said warmly, leaning forward on the table. "No, Meagan, I don't think you're an idiot. I think you're just the opposite."

"That just proves you don't know me very well," she said, making a show of modesty, but completely unable to hide her pleased smile.

"I know you went to college."

Meagan shrugged. "So?"

"So. I didn't. I barely finished high school."

She looked down and furrowed her brow. She wouldn't have guessed that about him. Actually, she hadn't given it any thought. But he ran a business; he appeared to be financially stable.

"OK. So I know you're a small town boy who struck out on his own in the big city. You have two sisters and one brother, and you were not academically motivated in your youth. What else?"

"Oh, no!" He leaned back in his seat as if applying brakes. "You've been asking all the questions. Now it's my turn."

She straightened her back, pleased at his interest. "OK."

"Is Caroline your only sibling?"

"Yes." She grinned.

"What did you study in college?"

Her grin widened. "Communication."

He paused and seemed to think about that for a minute.

"Anything else?"

He fixed a level stare on her, meeting and holding her gaze. "Where did you meet your ex-husband?"

Her grin faded. She felt suddenly as if she'd just had all the wind knocked out of her. Of course, he'd want to know about her marriage. It was only natural. But she felt so ill prepared to answer the question just now. She was having such a good time sitting across a candle lit table from this good-looking, nice man. The last person she wanted to think about right now was Kevin. But he'd asked. And to say she didn't want to talk about it would only seem melodramatic and moody. She sighed.

"I met him in college. He was studying journalism. He was all conviction and righteous indignation–like most twenty year olds. I was young. I thought he had fire." She gave him a rueful grin and a wry little laugh. "What did I know?"

"So you weren't happy?"

"Oh, we were happy." She tried to clear the hoarseness from her suddenly aching throat. "For about five years."

"Until?"

"Until I got pregnant." Tears burned and blurred her vision, but she tried to cover them by keeping her voice flat and looking down. It wasn't working. She took a sip of her tea.

"He didn't want a baby?"

She shook her head, venturing a glance at Bobby, grateful for the tenderness she heard in his voice. "No. But it's not all his fault. He told me before we got married that he didn't want to bring a child into this world. I just always figured he'd change his mind. Especially after..." Her voice broke, and she cleared her throat again. "Especially after..."

As hard as she tried she couldn't say it out loud. She couldn't articulate the fact that Kevin had known she was pregnant with his child, and he had left her because of it.

"Do you think he'll be back someday?"

"No. I don't think he'll ever come back. Not that it would matter. The divorce is over and done with. Has been since before Jay was even born."

"But if he did come back...?"

Bobby's voice was so low she almost asked him to repeat the question. But she didn't. She'd heard it, and asked it of herself many times.

She took a deep breath and smiled despite her regret. "I wouldn't take him back. I never should have married him. Neither of us were ready, we were totally wrong for each other."

He leaned forward. "In what way?"

She opened her mouth to explain, but apprehension stopped her short. This whole conversation had come around to the real reason her marriage had failed. And that same reason could stop this nebulous, wonderfully promising, relationship right here and now. But better now, than later.

"We were...'unequally yoked,' so to speak."

Something changed suddenly about his expression. Some sort of look registered on his face, something between surprise and disbelief, but she couldn't clearly define it, and he looked away when the waiter brought their entrees. As soon as they were alone he started questioning her again.

"'Unequally yoked' how?"

She took a deep breath, held it for a few seconds, then let it out quietly, laying her hands on the table for support as she did. "I'm a Christian, Bobby. Kevin wasn't. Still isn't, as far as I know."

He broke out into the widest grin she'd seen on him yet. But then he seemed to rein it in. "And that matters to you?"

"Yes." Heat rushed to her face at his amused expression, and she looked down hoping to cover her indignation.

"It matters to me, too, Meagan."

Her head snapped up, and she searched his face earnestly, trying to determine the exact meaning of his words by the expression in his eyes. "It does?"

He nodded. "I'm a Christian, too."

"You are?" Her voice sounded shocked and bewildered to her own ears. This was almost too good to be true! "You are?"

He laughed. "I am. Would you mind if we blessed the food?"

She felt her jaw slacken, but she held it firmly closed. "No. Of course I wouldn't mind."

He bowed his head, and she followed suit while he said a quick, quiet prayer of thanksgiving for their meal. Meagan glanced up as he prayed and silently uttered her own prayer of thanksgiving. It had absolutely nothing to do with the food.

❧❧

Meagan smiled as Bobby pulled his truck to a stop in front of her house and put it in park. At first she hadn't been sure they would have such a nice time. He seemed a little distant. But now she chalked his behavior up to nerves. He really was a remarkable man. Contentment mixed with disappointment now their date was over, but she comforted herself with the knowledge that he would ask her out again. All the signs pointed to it. Maybe he'd kiss her, too. The thought made her a little breathless.

"Well, here we are." Bobby's voice pierced the tranquil silence. "Did you have a nice time?"

She smiled encouragingly. "I did, Bobby. I had such a nice time. Thank you."

"It was my pleasure." He slipped from the truck and came around to open her door. She stepped out, and he closed the door behind her. Something in his attitude changed in the short walk from the pickup to the front door. The warmth she felt from him all evening evaporated, leaving a cool formality which seemed very odd. It made her doubt every good conclusion she'd already drawn about how well this night had gone.

"Would you like to come in for a few minutes?" She spoke quickly when they reached her door, hoping it would revive the dissipating enchantment of the evening, and extend their time together.

Bobby's gaze traveled the entire terrain of her face, coming to rest briefly on her mouth before he looked down at the keys he fumbled with. "No. I should get going. We both have to work tomorrow." He glanced back up and gave her a smile, but to Meagan it looked pained.

"OK," she said softly. "Thanks again for dinner. I had a great time."

He glanced up again quickly, then back down. "Me, too."

Then maybe you should ask me out again! It was all she could do to keep from snatching those keys from his hand and shouting the words at him. She'd just spent the last few hours getting to know this man. Granted, she was far from knowing him well, but she *did* know that he wasn't shy, and he had enough confidence not to turn into a jumble of nerves when the moment of truth with a woman arrived. He'd had a good time with her tonight. She'd told him stories and made him laugh and relax. And he'd talked more than she ever thought he would. She'd seen a whole other side of him. They enjoyed each other's company. And where she came from, that called for a second date.

Nerves weren't holding him back now. But something was.

"Maybe we could go see a movie next time." A little encouragement couldn't hurt. Whatever else happened, she did *not* want to spend the next couple of weeks sitting by the phone, jumping every time it rang, hoping he'd call.

That got a genuine smile from him, and he nodded. "That'd be nice."

She raised her chin. "Good. Then I'll be waiting for your call."

"Yes ma'am." A little half grin softened his features.

He didn't intend to kiss her. That much was obvious by the way he stood his ground over there on the opposite side of the small porch. She could live with that.

"Well." She took extra care not to focus her attention on his mouth. "Goodnight, then."

"Goodnight."

She opened the door and stepped inside, casting one last glance back at him. Then she closed it, leaning back against its solid mass, totally bewildered by that most bizarre, frustrating ending to an otherwise perfect first date.

5

No sooner had Meagan pressed her back against the door than Caroline peeked around the corner from the kitchen.

"So? How did it go?"

Meagan opened her mouth to answer, but closed it again. How *had* it gone? "I...I *think* it went OK." She pushed away from the door and dropped her purse into the nearest chair. Then she shrugged out of her sweater.

"What does *that* mean?" Caroline took a seat on the couch where a couple of her textbooks lay open.

A deeply felt sigh punctuated Meagan's words. "I don't know. I think it went OK. Things were a little awkward at first. But after we both warmed up a little, I thought we started having a good time."

Her sister narrowed her eyes. "So, he's as nice as you thought he'd be?"

She felt her expression soften as she smiled and nodded. "Yes. And, Caroline, he's a Christian!"

Although the words had come from her own mouth, she could still scarcely believe them. She knew from experience that any man she became involved with would have to share her faith. But she hadn't asked it of Bobby before tonight, not because she hadn't wondered, but because she had liked him so much she didn't want to know if he didn't. Not yet, anyway. She had wanted to be able to plead ignorance and spend a little time with him–even though that's exactly how it had started with Kevin.

"Did he kiss you?"

Meagan all but jumped at the question, then a delicious heat rushed to her face. Casting a sly grin at Caroline, she shook her head. "Not even close."

"So, maybe he didn't have such a good time?"

Meagan gasped in mock pain at the quip. "Or maybe he's a gentleman!"

Caroline smirked. "Well, which is it?"

Her shoulders sagged a little and she sighed again. "I don't know. He *seemed* to have a good time. We talked the whole time. But now that I think about it, we talked mostly about me." She paused and bit her lower lip, taking a seat next to her sister on the couch. "He just kept asking me questions. So I just kept on blabbering. But he seemed so interested. Then on the drive home he quit asking. He just quit talking."

"So on the way home he clammed up all of a sudden." Caroline raised a thoughtful finger to her chin. "Maybe he got nervous about asking you out again."

A blunt laugh escaped her. "Then why didn't he?"

"He didn't ask you out again?" Caroline's tone registered somewhere between amazement and shock.

"No. *I* basically asked *him* out–again!"

Caroline's brow furrowed as she stroked her chin. "What did he say?"

"He *said* it sounded like a good idea." She folded her hands in her lap and stared down at them. That *was* what he'd said, wasn't it? Suddenly she couldn't remember. If he *had* said it, how had he said it? What had been his tone of voice? She racked her brain trying to remember the exact way the conversation had gone. Had he sounded sincere, like he looked forward to seeing her again? Or had he simply been humoring her, like he didn't want to hurt her feelings, but had no intention of calling?

"Well, there you have it. He seemed like a straight talking sort of man to me. If he said it sounded like a good idea, then I'm sure that's what he meant."

Caroline's practical philosophy did little to ease her sudden anxiety. Meagan leaned forward and slid her shoes off, still obsessing over the exact words that had been exchanged and trying desperately to remember the tone of his voice and the look on his face.

"Don't wear yourself out worrying about it," Caroline added, returning her attention to the books. "He'll probably call tomorrow. If not sooner."

❧❦

Bobby made it as far as his truck before he turned around to glance back at Meagan's house. The warm glow from her front window beckoned, as the cool evening breeze, in seeming cooperation with the house, picked up at his back.

He should have told her.

Leaning back against the pickup, he drew a deep breath and let it out heavily, looking heavenward as if for advice. She deserved to know what kind of man he was, and he'd been on the verge of telling her as they stood together on her porch. The words had been right there on his lips, but then he looked into her eyes and saw how much she liked and trusted him.

And wasn't that why he'd come out here to

Lubbock anyway? To make a fresh start where no one knew him? Where he'd be free to change with no one questioning the legitimacy of it and wondering when he'd break down and ruin everything again?

He hadn't had a drink in over two and a half years, and he didn't intend to ever have one again. When he looked at Meagan he felt only tenderness and hope, no trace of violence or jealousy. He didn't feel like he had to convince her of his intent to do no harm. He could just be who he was. He'd never felt that way with a woman before.

He ran a hand across the back of his neck and looked down at his boots. With Audrey he'd always felt like he had to make the good times so much better, either to make up for the bad times, or to make her believe that he did possess some redeeming qualities. It had been that way from their very first date together. From the beginning he'd lived in fear that she'd kick him out of her life, even before the first time he'd shoved her. Everyone in town had known what he was, and there was every possibility someone would convince her that he was no good. Ultimately, he had done that all by himself.

Meagan looked at him and saw a decent, Christian man. When he looked at her, he saw no trace of fear that he might turn violent at any moment with little provocation. She had no reason to think he might. But if he went back up there to her front door and explained it all to her she would. He'd look into her eyes, and he'd see the wariness there. And then only if she didn't slam the door in his face and file for a restraining order.

Bobby shifted his weight as if his own body compelled him to action. He could say nothing about his past. He could let this relationship develop however it would, keeping his secret. But there was no way he could keep it from her forever. Sooner or later something would happen to bring it up. Maybe they'd run into someone from back home, or she'd meet his family, and it would come out. Then she really wouldn't trust him. Then she'd leave him for sure for lying to her.

If the relationship that was forming with this sweet, beautiful woman was going to end, better to end it now than later, before either one invested anything meaningful.

He pushed his weight off his truck and strode to her front door, losing what little confidence he had mustered with each step he took.

"Lord, I don't want to do this," he whispered when he got there.

But he had to. Trying to keep it a secret, covered up and out of sight, pretending it didn't exist, was something he would have done back then. And Meagan deserved to know. She deserved the opportunity to make the decision herself, before anything bad even had the chance to happen.

He took a fortifying breath, raised his hand, and knocked on her door.

∂◦∽

Meagan saw Caroline start, same as she did, when the knock sounded. She jumped up and hurried to the door to take a look through the peep hole. Through it she saw Bobby's distorted form standing on the other side of the door. Her heart pounded wildly.

"It's him!" she whispered.

Caroline snapped her books shut and gathered them into her arms. "I'm out of here!"

"Wait! What should I do? What do you think he wants? How do I look?"

"Open the door and ask him what he wants. And you look the same as you did ten minutes ago." Caroline shot her a pointed look. "Answer it!" Then she turned and hurried down the hall to her room.

Meagan smoothed her hair and pushed a few fallen tendrils behind her ears. She straightened her skirt and took a deep, calming breath. Then she unlocked the door and pulled it open.

Bobby stood with those keys still clutched in his hands, just like he had when she'd come inside a few moments ago. Only now the expression on his face made him look rather like he'd just run over her dog.

"What's wrong?" She opened the door wide as an invitation.

He hesitated for a second or two, then he stepped across the threshold. "I...I need to talk to you. There's something I need to say."

Her brows shot up. "There is?"

He turned to face her as she closed the door, and she saw him swallow just before he cleared his throat.

"Would you like some tea?"

"Um, yeah." He looked around. "That'd be nice. Is Caroline still here?"

"She's gone to bed." Meagan headed for the kitchen. When she returned with two glasses of iced tea, he'd taken a seat in one of the chairs instead of the sofa. She set his glass down on the table beside him and then sat down on the couch. He sat, leaning forward with elbows resting on knees and fingers clasped, hardly seeming to notice her presence in the room.

"Bobby?" She leaned forward trying to regain his attention. "You had something you wanted to say?"

He looked at her briefly, then picked up his glass for a sip. "Yeah." He took a deep breath and leaned forward again, studying the glass in his hands as if he expected it to do something. "Yeah. I just... There's just..."

"Bobby, it's OK." She smiled warmly when his voice trailed off. "I'm probably not going to throw you out of my house for whatever it is you have to say."

He pressed against the back of the chair and stared with shock, then amazement, registering on his face. He laughed, running a hand over his eyes and then through his hair. He sat there laughing, but the anguish she heard in his voice gave her chills. She took a sip of her own tea to cover the apprehension that suddenly saturated her mind.

"Oh, Meagan," he said at length. "If you only knew."

"Knew what?"

He leaned forward again and studied her for a long moment. Then he took a breath. "I've only been a Christian for a couple of years."

She wanted to relax, as if that was all he had to tell her. But she had no doubt by the look on his face, his tense posture, and this long, charged pause, that more would follow. She didn't have a clue what this was all about and it was beginning to frighten her a little.

"Before that..." He stalled again and shook his head, obviously deciding to start over. "Remember when I told you about my little hometown? How nobody's business was a secret?"

She nodded.

"And remember how you asked if I left to get away from everyone who knew my business?"

She blinked, trying to remember if she'd asked him that, but nodded anyway.

"Well, that's exactly why I left. After I got saved, I tried hard to prove to everyone how much I wanted to change who I was. I wanted them to believe that I could become a better man. And a few were willing to allow that, with God's grace and a little time, I could. But just a few. And everybody else just kept watching, and waiting...most folks there couldn't let me change—in *their* minds. I was what I was, and there was no changing it."

Meagan felt her brows knit together as she listened and tried to understand him.

"Change? In what way, Bobby?" She shook her head wondering what on earth could have been so bad. "So you were a new Christian. We all were at some point. Are you sure–"

He shook his head again and held up a hand to stop the flow of her words.

"I'm not what you think I am."

Her heart picked up its pace and her hands and feet went cold.

Lord, protect me. Her panic stricken, silent prayer went up as she began entertaining visions of the last murder mystery she'd watched on late-night television.

"And what do I think you are?" Her voice sounded calm, if quieter than usual. That was good.

He smiled genuinely, fondly. "You think I'm decent and good."

"If you're not those things, what are you?"

He sighed and took a breath as if to speak, but

then he stopped again.

"Bobby, I'm sorry, but I need you to come to the point because this conversation is totally unnerving me! Just tell me what it is you have to say."

"OK." He sounded determined. "OK. I haven't had a drink in over two years."

Her jaw dropped, and she narrowed her eyes, almost wanting to choke him for building this conversation in such a way that she had entertained the fleeting notion that he could be a serial killer. "You haven't had a drink...? And so before that you were an alcoholic?"

His breathing seemed to stop, and he just stared at her for a moment. He struggled, but finally opened his mouth to speak. "I...I um...I still have a hard time admitting it. I don't like to hear myself say it out loud. I'd rather say I just used to drink a little too much. But yes. I was–I guess I am–an...an alcoholic."

All her tension dissipated in one long sigh, and she smiled. "But you haven't had a drink in two years?"

This wasn't so bad. OK, so he was a recovering alcoholic. There were plenty of worse things to be. And he was well on his way to recovery if it had been two years.

He nodded. "I also lived with a woman for six years."

She grinned wider, thinking he had an unreasonably low opinion of himself considering all these transgressions were committed before he came to know the Lord. "And I'm divorced."

"But I..." He looked down at his hands which he had clasped together. "But I wasn't married to the woman I lived with. And I, um...I frequently mistreated her."

Meagan's grin vanished as that statement sank in, and all the possible meanings began to tear through her mind. She desperately fought the almost overwhelming urge to scoot further down the couch away from him. "In what way?"

He swallowed. "In exactly the way you're probably imagining, judging by the way you're looking at me."

She glanced away as heat flooded her face.

"I shoved her." He looked down and swallowed hard. "Slapped her, punched her, kicked her." He winced visibly with each act he added to his list and he stared unwaveringly at his knees. "I yelled at her a lot, called her hateful names." When he hazarded a glance at her, his voice sounded almost pleading. "I was always at least half drunk, Meagan. When I was sober I never laid a hand on her that way."

"Why are you telling me this?" Her voice, little more than a whisper, almost broke as tears rushed to her eyes.

"Because I thought you deserved to know. Before this went any further, I thought you ought to know." He paused and she stole a tentative glance in his direction. His expression looked so pained and remorseful, almost as if he'd done all those things to her personally. "I'll understand if you want me to leave now. And if you don't want to see me again."

He stood and she did, too. When he started for the door, she stayed well clear of him, making no effort to stop him. What else could she do? Her whole heart refused to believe what he'd just told her. She'd seen no trace of evidence that he possessed the capability of battering a woman. But wasn't that the way everyone always said it happened? And here he stood, in her living room, admitting it openly.

When he got to the door he stopped and turned to her, waiting, silently pleading for her to tell him it was OK, and she wanted him to stay. That she knew that wasn't him anymore. But she couldn't.

She whispered hoarsely through her tears. "I have a son. A little boy. I just can't–"

"I understand." He interrupted. "If I were you, I'd make the same choice."

How can this be? Meagan wanted to scream the words. How could this man–this decent, honest, vulnerable man who stood beside her now–be capable of such a thing? If this was true, why did she feel absolutely no check in her spirit about any possible danger in becoming involved with him? If he was such a bad guy, why couldn't she tell?

"Bobby...?"

He looked up at her, his expression lit with sudden hope.

Are you sure? She wanted to ask. *Are you sure you're remembering it all correctly?*

"Thanks again for dinner," she said lamely instead.

He looked down and nodded, clearly deflated. "I won't call you, Meagan. I won't come around and bother you. So don't worry about your safety. I would never hurt you. I would rather die than ever raise my hand to a woman again."

With that he opened her front door and stepped out.

"Goodbye, Bobby," she said. Then she pushed the door closed and locked it.

Again, she leaned against its solid wooden

strength. He had said he wouldn't call or come around. She squeezed her eyes shut and pressed both hands to them as if the gesture could stop the rush of ambivalent emotion that besieged her. Not two minutes after he'd admitted to regularly battering his live-in girlfriend he'd told her he'd never hurt her. He'd said he'd rather die.

"Lord, help me." She whispered the desperate prayer, as it dawned on her that she believed him.

❧

That had gone just as badly as he feared it would. But as he left her house he'd still been standing. He'd still been OK, until he'd heard the key turn in the lock between them, effectively crushing any hope he'd had of ever truly being free from his past. It was the sound of that bolt sliding into place that had made him want to drop to his knees and howl his anger and remorse and frustration straight up to God. Instead, he'd let his shoulders sag beneath the weight of what he was, and he'd trudged the distance to his truck and driven home to his sparsely-furnished, one-bedroom apartment.

He hated apartment living. Hated being surrounded by people who belonged to rowdy families, and had friends that would stop by for visits making noise until all hours of the night. In the unit above him right now was a group that would occasionally burst out in laughter.

Bobby sat on the edge of the bed in his dark bedroom, and buried his head in his hands.

"Why, Father?" he prayed. "Why have You brought me here? Right now I'd rather be a total outsider in my own hometown, drunk and disorderly, than all alone way out here where no one knows me or cares enough to even talk bad about me."

Another shout of voices combined in laughter stirred the darkness around him. He raised his head and his gaze to the ceiling.

"What do I do now? Am I supposed to just get up and go to work, same as I've done every day for the last year? And just come home and watch T.V. until bed time, then go to bed so I can just get up and do it again tomorrow? Is that all there is for me here?"

More boisterous voices floated down from above, but that was all.

Bobby pulled off his boots and left them right where they landed beside his bed, then he laid back and propped his head on his pillows, folding his arms across his chest. He tried to swallow the ache that began forming in his throat, but it didn't budge. Then he heard it–the still small voice he had come to rely on way out here, so far from home.

Wait.

6

Walking the two block distance between Jay's daycare center and the salon had become routine. More and more, Meagan found herself using the short time it took to get from one place to the other to dwell on the hardships that consistently plagued her lately. This morning, as she headed down to the salon after dropping Jay off, all she could think about was that he had not adjusted well in the month he'd been in this new situation.

Meagan had confidence in the small, church-affiliated preschool, but Jay seemed overly shy all of a sudden, and reluctant to let go of her legs and join the other kids when they arrived each morning. At first she'd just chalked the behavior up to the new surroundings and people. But more than a month had passed, and he seemed no more accustomed to the place now than on the first day. He'd been sick twice in the past few weeks, too. He'd hardly ever been sick before.

Tears blurred her vision.

Why, Lord? Why do I have to keep taking him to a daycare center when I want to be the one taking care of him? He's not happy. I'm not happy. Why does it have to be this way? What can I do?

Meagan pulled open the salon door, so absorbed in her thoughts that she didn't see the man sitting in the waiting area as she passed through. But she recognized his voice the instant he spoke her name.

"Meagan?"

She spun around, then tried to blink the tears out of her eyes. Bobby stood on the other side of the counter.

"Bobby! Hi."

He smiled tentatively. "Hi."

For a few nights after their date, she had cried herself to sleep over the inherent unfairness of the whole situation between them. If God hadn't wanted her to become attracted to this man, why had He brought him across her path? Why couldn't anything ever just be simple?

She smiled back, though she felt no joy in it.

"I could use a trim." He ran one hand over the top of his head. "I was just on my way to work, and I thought I'd take a chance stopping by to see if you could fit me in."

She nodded. "Sure. I don't have anybody scheduled for about thirty minutes. Come on back." She cast him a sideways glance and did her best to grin. "Did you just want your regular trim today? Or do you feel like having a shampoo, too?"

"Just a trim." His answer was curt as he took a seat in her chair.

Meagan bit her lip. She should have known he wouldn't appreciate the teasing reminder of his last appointment with her. Things were different between them, now. She settled a cape over his shoulders, fastening it around his neck. She worked as quickly as she could, and not another word passed between them until she handed him a mirror so he could inspect her work.

"Looks good. Thanks."

She unfastened the cape and lifted it off of him, then laid a hand on his shoulder before he could stand. He looked up and met her gaze in the mirror.

"You could have called for an appointment, Bobby," she said softly. "I know the reason you just dropped by is probably because you were afraid I wouldn't take your call. But I would."

He searched her tearful gaze for several seconds before he finally nodded and stood up. Although he reached for his wallet, she could feel his continued examination of her profile after she turned to straighten up her station. From the corner of her eye she saw him hold out a few folded bills as he tucked his wallet into his back pocket. She turned to receive it without making eye contact.

"Thanks," she muttered.

When he didn't move to leave right away, she glanced cautiously up at him.

"You gonna be OK?"

She nodded and blinked, causing tears to spill over. "I just hate that I've hurt your feelings."

He smiled reassuringly at that and leaned back against her cabinet. "Meagan, you were crying when you got here. I'm not egotistical enough to believe that it was because of me."

She shook her head and reached across her counter for a tissue. "It's Jay."

His expression turned serious. "Is everything OK?"

"He's fine," she said quickly. "He just hates the little daycare he has to go to." She sniffed and felt her face contort in anticipation of the sob she knew was coming. She reached for her chair and sat down, trying to cover it, but the sob came anyway.

"Every morning he cries when I take him. He cries, and the teachers there have to pry his little arms from around my neck, and he begs to go with me. I almost can't take it. Every morning. He's in tears, I'm in tears..."

All she wanted was to quit this job and stay home with her baby. *She* wanted to take care of him. She wanted to enjoy him instead of always having to rush around getting him ready for daycare in the morning and then bed at night. He was growing up so fast, and she was missing it while she stood on her feet all day cutting other people's hair.

"What happened to the babysitter that lived just down the street from you?"

"She moved a while back." Meagan sniffed.

"Don't your parents live around here? What about them?"

"They both still work." She dabbed at her eyes, wiped her nose, and took a shaky breath, commanding control of her emotions again. "And then there's my ex, who's filed for bankruptcy. Leaving me with about fifteen thousand dollars of unpaid credit card bills. The collection agencies won't stop calling. You know, I can take hard times, but this...this just never seems to end."

She took another deep breath and rubbed the back of her neck, willing her tensed muscles and clenched jaw to relax. She'd said too much. There was no way he cared about her problems now, after she'd rejected him. "Anyway..." She shook her head and glanced back up at his shocked face. "Things have been a little rough lately. I'm sorry, Bobby," she added hastily as the bell on the front door opened and Alicia strolled in. "I shouldn't have unloaded on you that way.

Especially since..."

He held up a hand to silence her. "Don't apologize, Meagan. We can at least be friends, right?"

Weary tears threatened again, and the impulse to fling herself into his arms and have a good cry on his shoulder seized her quite suddenly. It would be almost blissfully comforting to feel his arms around her while she leaned on his quiet strength. To hear him say softly in her ear that everything was going to be all right. She ached with that need.

Despite all that, she merely nodded, accepting his offer of platonic friendship. "Of course we can."

He pushed his weight off the cabinet. "Call me if you need anything. OK? I've been through my share of hard times. I know what it's like. I know that sometimes having someone to talk to makes all the difference."

She smiled weakly and nodded her thanks.

Alicia came to stand beside her after he'd turned to go and together they watched him walk out to his pickup. Had it really been only two weeks since he'd admitted his past to her and she'd sent him away? Seeing him now, it felt like forever. And it felt totally *wrong*. Meagan frowned. Was it possible that she'd misunderstood everything he'd said? She just couldn't reconcile the man he said he'd been with the man who had just stood quietly listening to her problems and then made a sincere, undemanding offer of friendship.

Meagan balled her hands into fists, fighting the impulse to run after Bobby as he stepped up into his truck and pulled the door closed. He'd told her to call him if she needed anything. But if she let him drive away now, she'd never call him. And he wouldn't call her either, except for a haircut appointment. That much she knew. And then they'd fall back into their previous "acquainted" relationship, only it would be awkward for them both. In a few months' time he'd find someone else to cut his hair, and then she'd never see him again. Was that what she wanted?

Call me if you need anything. OK? That was the thought that occurred as she bolted for the door when she heard him start the engine. The words echoed as she pushed the door open and rushed outside. She needed something alright. She couldn't explain it, but she knew it in her soul. She needed him. She wanted *him*.

The gears shifted as Bobby turned to back out of his parking space.

"Bobby, *wait!*" Meagan waved and ran across the sidewalk toward him.

He shifted back into park and lowered his window.

"Bobby, I..." Meagan stopped. Heat rushed to her face. She'd almost blurted out the last thing that went through her mind as she raced outside. That she needed him. That she was sorry for sending him away the other night. That no matter what he'd done in the past, God had changed him, and he deserved another chance.

The truck on Bobby's passenger side began to back out of its space, and the motion of it threw her off balance. Or maybe it was the pace of her heartbeat making her dizzy. All she knew was that he sat there now, one arm draped over the steering wheel, returning her hopeful smile as if he could read her mind. And deep inside her heart she knew that giving him a chance was right.

The world seemed to stand still around them. But

somewhere, in some vague, recessed part of her brain she heard the squeal of rubber on asphalt as someone's brakes locked up. Then came the sound of twisting, buckling steel, and shattering glass. That was the last thing she heard.

∂∽

Voices floated and drifted around the room, seemingly from her right, then her left, then from right above her. Gradually her mind began to focus, and as her eyes fluttered open she could clearly distinguish three quiet voices; two male, one female. Meagan still couldn't quite make out what they were saying through the fog in her brain. But then, as her eyes opened completely, she faced a brand new challenge in identifying her location.

She recognized the form standing on her right with its back to her. "Mom?"

Her mother spun around and reached for her hands. Her father stepped closer and peered over her mother's shoulder.

"Dad? Am I in a hospital?"

"Yes, honey. You were in an accident."

"Am I OK?"

"Well, you have a broken leg. And you bumped your head pretty good."

"Then why doesn't anything hurt?" She shifted in her bed, intending to sit up a little, then realized she'd spoken too soon. The pain started as a little pinpoint epicenter in the middle of her head and spread like a wave to cover the rest instantly. She groaned and leaned her head back against the pillows.

"Where's Jay? Is he OK?"

"He's fine." Her mother sat down beside the bed. "He's still at daycare. I'm going to go get him in a little while."

"He hates it there."

"I know, hon, but since he was already there, I thought it was the best place for him while we sorted all this out."

"You say I was in an accident?"

"Meagan, I'm Doctor Stirling." A man in green scrubs stepped into her sight line and looked at her compassionately before leaning in closer to check her eyes. "Can you tell me the last thing you remember?"

She blinked when he finished and closed her eyes against the pain in her head. "I was at work. I was standing outside talking to Bobby. He was in his truck." She caught her breath and her eyes flew open wide. "What happened? I don't know what happened after that. Is Bobby OK?"

The doctor grinned down at her. "If you mean the guy out in the hall, he's fine. He's been waiting around all morning for you to wake up. You feel up to seeing him?"

She nodded, then winced. "Is there any way I could get something for this headache?"

Dr. Stirling nodded and turned for the door. "I'll see what I can do."

A moment later Bobby appeared at the door. He looked around as if unsure he'd be allowed to enter. But when his gaze caught hers, he stepped across the threshold decisively. He pulled a chair right up next to the bed and sat down, studying her face intensely.

"Bobby, what happened?" She raised a hand to touch the small bandage just above his left eyebrow. It seemed that he leaned into her touch a little, but she was so dizzy, she could be mistaken about that.

"The guy parked on the other side of me pulled about halfway out and got hit pretty hard from behind. It knocked him into my truck, and my truck into...um...you."

"Are you hurt?" She withdrew her hand and tried to shift her position to get a better look at him.

He shook his head. "Just needed a few stitches. I'm not even sure what I hit my head on."

"Talk about a freak accident." Meagan had to concentrate hard to shift her gaze to her father as he spoke.

"Bobby, these are my parents, Patrick and Mary Anne Morrison."

"We've met, hon." Her dad patted her hand. "You've been out awhile."

Meagan swallowed and cleared her throat. "Who called y'all?"

"Your friend, Alicia." Her mom poured a cup of water from a decanter on a rolling tray beside her, and handed it to Meagan. "She found our number in your phone."

Meagan furrowed her brow. Everything they said made perfect sense. She'd been in an accident. She was in the hospital. She was going to be OK. Everything was under complete control. But her mind still swayed back and forth in foggy confusion, and she wanted to close her eyes and drift off again.

"Jay..." she began.

"Your Dad and I are going to get him right now." Her mother rose from the bedside chair, gave her a gentle hug, then gathered her purse and sweater. "We'll bring him here to see you."

"Thanks, Mom."

Her mom blew her a kiss, then her folks disappeared down the corridor. She shifted her gaze to Bobby, who had started picking at a corner of the bandage on his forehead.

"So, you met my parents while I was unconscious."

He glanced up and smiled. "Probably not the best of circumstances. Now they already think I can't take care of you."

Meagan blinked. *What?*

"I'm sorry." He cleared his throat and glanced away. "I shouldn't assume...it's just that when you came out of the shop to talk to me, I thought..." His voice trailed off and he shook his head with a dismissive smile. "Never mind."

"You thought right, Bobby." She reached over and covered his hand with hers. "I came out to stop you. I was afraid if you left, I'd never see you again."

His strong fingers closed around hers. "And you wanted to see me again?"

She smiled. "Yes."

"Even after everything I told you about myself?"

"Don't sound so skeptical about it. I'm too befuddled not to second guess everything right now. Besides which, I've got a few problems of my own."

"OK." He gave her fingers a gentle squeeze. "OK. You need to rest, and we can talk about all this later."

"Time for your medicine." Meagan started as a nurse came in with a little cup of pills.

"Ooh, good thing. My leg is starting to hurt, too." She smiled and swallowed a few little pills which looked remarkably like over the counter pain relievers.

"It's broken," the nurse said.

Meagan shot a wry, half amused grin at Bobby as

she tried to shift again to alleviate the throbbing in her leg. "Well, I guess that would explain it."

❧

"So, can I be the first one to sign your cast?"

Meagan looked up from her magazine to find Caroline standing in the doorway of her hospital room. "Sorry, you're too late." She wiggled her toes, drawing attention to a few childishly scrawled lines near her ankle.

"I see Jay's already been at it."

"With a little encouragement from his grandpa. What are you doing here?" Meagan closed the magazine she'd been reading and laid it aside.

"You know me. Any excuse to skip a few classes." Caroline perched on the edge of the chair beside Meagan's bed.

"Be serious! It's a long drive from Austin to Lubbock."

"I didn't drive, I flew."

Meagan raised her brows. "I don't recall having enough money when I was in college to just hop on a plane and get away for the weekend."

Caroline grinned. "Times have changed."

"Evidently."

"So, what happened?"

"Oh," Meagan waved a dismissive hand. "Some kind of freakish accident."

Caroline shook her head. "I know all about that. I mean, what happened with Bobby? You two are together now?"

Meagan shrugged. "I think so. It's kind of hard to tell, things being what they are right now. He's been here every minute he could spare, but between the doctors and nurses, and Mom and Dad, there haven't been too many private moments to discuss it."

"And to think, it just took him squashing you with his truck to make it all finally happen."

"It was an accident." The comment sounded sharp, and she instantly regretted her defensiveness. She hadn't explained to Caroline the reason she sent Bobby away before. When Caroline had asked, tears had pooled and she told her sister she didn't want to talk about it. She still didn't. But obviously the information she had regarding Bobby's past already colored her behavior where he was concerned.

"I know." Caroline sounded as if she hadn't caught Meagan's protective tone. But she continued to study her with narrowed eyes until, thankfully, a light knock sounded on the door.

"Come in," Meagan called.

The door swung open, and Bobby peeked around the corner. "Did somebody order room service?"

Meagan grinned, almost forgetting Caroline was in the room.

"Oh. Hi, Caroline." Bobby stopped short as soon as he stepped fully into the room. "I'd have brought more if I'd known you were gonna be here."

"It smells like fried chicken." Meagan motioned him closer. "Caroline can share mine."

"I better eat all of yours. The doctor isn't going to like you eating fried chicken."

Meagan shrugged. "I have a broken leg, not clogged arteries."

"Still," Caroline mused. "This is a hospital, and it seems to me there should be rules. I'll just go tell the nurse to bring you a tray of nice hospital food. For

Moving On

your own good."

"They know better." Meagan opened her box of chicken and picked off a piece of the breading. "Bobby keeps bringing me food. Most people lose weight in the hospital. But I've probably gained five pounds in two days."

Caroline snagged a couple of fries. "Boy, you must really feel guilty."

Bobby looked down at one of the sodas he'd brought. "It was *my* truck that broke her leg."

"Bobby! I'm kidding! I know you didn't break her leg on purpose. Who would do something like that?"

His smile faded, and his jaw set.

"Mmm. This is good." Caroline chattered on, not noticing the change in him.

"Hey!" Meagan gave her sister's hand a playful slap. "That's mine."

"You said I could share."

"OK, Miss English major, shall we get the dictionary and look up the exact definition of the word 'share'?"

Caroline grinned the very same grin that got her out of every ounce of trouble she'd ever been in. Meagan returned an indulgent smile and centered the tray between them. Bobby pulled a chair up and joined them.

"So, when do you get to go home?" Caroline looked from her to Bobby.

"Tomorrow." She dragged her gaze from Bobby's to look at her sister, whom she was always glad to see. But she so wanted to talk to him alone. *Tomorrow.*

Tomorrow she'd be getting out of here. Tomorrow she'd be going home to start the next phase of her life. There was no way to tell where this new relationship

91

would go. She slid her gaze back to his face. He was laughing at something Caroline said, which Meagan hadn't heard. Gradually his laughter faded to that amazing, wide smile of his. He glanced at her, and his expression softened.

No, there was no way of telling just where they'd go together. But they'd officially start heading that direction tomorrow.

7

"You sure you're OK to do this?"

"Yes, Bobby." Meagan indulged his solicitude with a grin and an affectionate tousle of his hair. "In fact, if we waited any longer to do this I'd ruin a good pair of scissors. Look at how thick your hair has gotten!"

He reached up and ran his own hand through it.

"You should have had it cut two weeks ago."

"I wanted to make sure you were OK to be up on your feet again."

She grinned and crossed to her kitchen sink, filling her spray bottle when she got there. "I've been up on my feet half days for three weeks now."

"I know." He sounded mildly defensive. "I just wanted to be sure."

"You could have had Alicia do it."

The quivery, burning soreness of overtaxed muscles hounded already as she made the simple journey back across her kitchen to where Bobby sat with a cape fastened around his neck.

"I didn't want Alicia to do it," he grumbled as she sprayed his hair down with the water, parting it here and there to make sure it got a thorough soaking. "I'm used to the way you do it."

"Admit it." She grabbed a section of his hair and gave it playful tug. "You just wanted a free haircut."

"Ow!" He chuckled and raised a hand to where she'd pulled his hair. "I'm starting to get my feelings hurt. Here I am looking out for you, trying to take care of you, and you accuse me of only wanting a free haircut. What kind of man do you take me for?"

She giggled at his mock indignation. "Ulterior motives or no, you've taken excellent care of me. And for that I thank you. With a free haircut."

Meagan rubbed her back and then set to work on him, her thoughts keeping time with the snipping of her scissors. He *had* taken good care of her. After she'd settled back in at home he came straight here when he got off work, as had her mom for a week or so.

Her mother thought it might be best for Jay to go on to his daycare center during the days, since Meagan would be home alone and unable to get around well. But Meagan insisted that he stay home with her. The first few days were rough, and had her thinking that her mom's advice might have been right. But she adjusted, and had actually become quite agile on her crutches, though the weight of the cast threw her off balance frequently.

Meagan shifted her position. Now the absence of its weight was throwing her off balance–not that she wasn't glad to have the cast gone.

By her second week at home, Meagan had adapted to the point that her mom felt comfortable with a couple of phone calls a day, and visits every two or three days. But Bobby came over every evening.

She ran a comb through his hair to check her progress on his cut so far. Shorter. Bobby looked good with short hair. He looked good with longer hair, too. *Let's face it, the man just plain looks good.* She sighed, combing and snipping, and letting her mind wander to the first night she'd been alone with him.

It had been clear that Bobby hadn't spent much time around kids. He tried to help her get Jay ready for bed. Bless his heart, he'd really tried. But he didn't have a clue what to do. She smiled at the memory.

But once they were finally totally alone, the discomfort between them settled in immediately. For a solid hour all she could imagine were all the possible ways he might have mistreated his last girlfriend. Each scenario she played out in her mind became more violent and frightening than the last, in response to the all-consuming awareness that she and Jay were totally alone in the house with him, and she incapacitated with a broken leg.

But Bobby never laid a hand on her. Not once, in any way.

In the past six or so weeks she'd touched him plenty. Just like she was doing now. She might lose her balance and reach out to him for support. He'd always respond, reaching back to steady her, but only when she initiated the contact.

She thought of them as a couple in an odd sort of way. But maybe she shouldn't just assume he felt the same way. Maybe that's why he seemed so hesitant to show her any physical affection. Maybe he didn't think of them in that way yet.

"You sure turned quiet all of a sudden." Bobby's warm, deep, relaxed voice called her out of her thoughts. She smiled and tilted his head forward gently for a better angle on her finishing touches. "What's on your mind?"

"I was just thinking how good it feels not to have a cast on my leg."

"Guess you can get your life back to normal

again."

She tilted his head back again and began to comb his hair into its usual style. "I hope that doesn't mean you'll stop coming by in the evenings."

He didn't respond as she unsnapped the cape and lifted it away from him.

Brushing bits of hair off his shoulders, he stood up, then moved the chair back to its place under her kitchen table.

Please, oh please, say something, she wanted to beg. *Please don't give up on us before we even have a chance.*

He stood for a long moment, gripping the back of the chair with both hands. What she wouldn't give to be able to read his mind right now. But all she could do was guess.

Maybe he really didn't think of them as a couple. Maybe in the past several weeks, as they'd talked hours on end, he'd come to the conclusion that he didn't like her after all. Maybe he was trying to find the words to tell her he wouldn't be coming by in the evenings anymore, now that she was back up on her feet.

"What's on *your* mind?" She heard the troubled tremor in her voice and cringed inwardly.

He sighed and ran a hand across the back of his neck. Then he uttered a nervous laugh. "This was easier when you had that cast on your leg."

"What was?"

"This." He swept his hand across the room, and then back and forth between them. "Being here. With you."

"Oh." Understanding dawned along with a slow smile. "And now I'm not such an invalid. There's a chance we might relate to each other normally. You might even feel led to act on an impulse to touch me."

He leveled his steady gaze on her and smiled a little ruefully.

"Am I right?" She stepped closer to him, ignoring how her legs and back protested that she ought to just sit down.

He nodded and looked down. He looked ashamed. "The last woman I touched..." His voice trailed off, and he glanced at her.

"Yes." Meagan stepped closer still, closing the distance between them to half an arm's length. "You told me already. And now I don't want to talk about it anymore."

"I just want you to be sure–"

"Bobby." She interrupted him softly. "I've made my choice. It's subject to change based on how you treat me. And I don't mind telling you if you ever *mis*treat me, I have a few relatives who won't think twice about...well, let's just say they won't approve."

The tension in his shoulders relaxed, but he still had a white-knuckled grip on the back of the chair with one hand.

"People can change, Bobby. I believe that with all my heart. You've told me what you were back then. But all I know is what you are now. I'm sure."

For a long moment he just stood there, studying her features, his grip on the chair tightening, then relaxing. Finally, she held her hand out to him. His Adam's apple drifted up and then down as he swallowed hard. Slowly he moved. Then she felt the strong, solid warmth of his work-toughened skin as he closed his hand around her own and intertwined his fingers with hers.

She smiled. "See there. It's not so hard."

But it was. Her heart lurched at the realization that his hesitancy to touch her had nothing whatsoever to do with her. It wasn't that he didn't think of them as a couple yet. Probably more than anything, that's just what he wanted. But he didn't trust himself to be with her. He was still convicting himself for crimes committed in past years, against someone else, and for which the price had already been paid.

His grip on her fingers tightened with what was probably a natural desire to pull her into his arms. She felt the same desire. But a moment later his hold on her slackened almost to nothing, and she feared he might let go. But then it tightened again and he tenderly caressed her skin with his thumb.

He looked down at their joined hands. He was holding back for her sake, and she wouldn't push him. But a little encouragement might not hurt. She offered her other hand.

He took it into his, then he swallowed and cleared his throat. "Can I..." He paused and raised his gaze to hers. "Can I kiss you?"

She opened her mouth to answer, but the intensity of his expression silenced her. This was not the sort of man she figured typically asked permission before he kissed a woman. But his need for it now was clear. All she could do was nod.

With one step Bobby closed what remained of the distance between them. His gaze traveled the whole landscape of her face, and, oh, the way he was looking at her now–like she was a precious treasure behind glass, to be admired but never touched, unique in every way, priceless, invaluable. No man had ever looked at her this way. It took her breath away.

He raised one hand and pressed his palm to her

cheek. Meagan leaned into his touch, her eyes closing of their own volition, and she thought she heard his breath catch, but she couldn't seem to open her eyes to check his reaction. Her whole world at this moment was his touch. How long had it been? How many years since a man had touched her like this? It took some effort to fill her lungs, but somehow she continued to breathe. She could feel the steady rise and fall of her chest.

"Mmmm." She heard the soft sound of her own voice as a breath strummed across her vocal chords, producing the sound without her consent.

Finally she lifted her heavy lids to look at him again. And there it was. That same look, like she was just too good to be true. *This is the one*, something inside her whispered. *He's the one.*

Slowly Bobby moved closer, sliding his hand from her cheek, around her neck, to cradle her head. His fingers wove themselves into her hair, and he bent his head toward hers, stopping a mere inch before his mouth touched hers.

Sheer agony. That's what waiting for this kiss was like. Sweet, thrilling, exquisite agony. Her every muscle had tensed, every sense heightened. From the look on his face, to the warm pressure of his hand on her neck sending a steady stream of shivers down her spine, to the sound of their deep, increasingly ragged breaths, to the scent of his cologne, this coming kiss was her whole world right now. All that was left was to taste it.

Bobby raised his gaze from her mouth to her eyes, then he smiled. *You won't be disappointed.* That's what his smile seemed to say.

I know, is what she hoped her answering smile told

him.

Then the warm softness of his mouth covered hers, gently, feather-light at first. Then again, firmer, closer. A third time, closer still, and deeper. *So* worth the wait.

She melted in his arms, sliding her hands up the length of his chest, feeling the muscles there tense under her touch, then around his neck. Bobby slid both arms around her, tightening his hold. And a good thing it was, because all her senses told her she was floating.

She heard the sound of her own voice again, but it sounded far away. It sounded foreign to her ears, hoarse with rising passion and abandon.

"Baby, you feel so good." His voice was ragged and hoarse as hers when he spoke between kisses, and something about the sound of it helped restore a small measure of sanity. That and the sudden desire to feel his hands on her in a much more intimate way. And that thought shocked every ounce of sense back into focus.

Meagan slid her hands back down to his chest and pressed firmly enough against him that he understood she wanted him to stop. She felt his embrace weaken and she reluctantly pulled her mouth from his. He stood, breathless as she, blinking as if he'd just snapped out of a trance and didn't quite remember where he was. Then he broke into a provocative grin.

"I...I feel like maybe I should apologize." He leaned toward her and stole one soft kiss, and then another. "But I'm just not sorry."

She glanced down, a smile touching her swollen lips, unable to meet his gaze. If she did she feared what little composure remained would disintegrate to nothing, and she'd throw herself back into his arms.

"How about some tea?"

He coughed and cleared his throat. "I guess it'll do."

She nodded and backed out of his arms slowly, just a little at a time, testing the soundness of the ground beneath her. The embarrassment would kill her if her wobbly knees buckled on the way to the refrigerator and he had to come pick her up off the floor.

๛๛

Jay's delighted, high-pitched squeal rang across the shady playground causing others to glance his direction and smile.

"No! Stop!" he cried through his giggles.

"Oh, you want me to stop, do you?" Bobby drew his hands away from the toddler's rib cage, careful to keep them poised like tickle claws.

"Yes! Stop!"

Bobby finally put his hands down. "OK, OK."

Jay lay perfectly still on the quilt Meagan had spread over the grass. He panted and huffed and puffed, not seeming to notice the glance his mother and his attacker exchanged.

After catching his breath, Jay bounced up onto his knees and squealed. "Again!"

"Again?" Bobby grinned. "But you said to stop."

"Again!" Jay lunged at Bobby, wrapping his arms around his neck, crawling onto his back. "Again!"

She watched as Jay tried, with little finesse, to poke and tickle Bobby's sides. Bobby lay face down on the quilt, laughing more at the enthusiastic effort than the actual effect. He caught her glance as he rolled over and began his next assault, to Jay's exuberant squeals.

She sighed and began pulling their sandwiches out of the picnic basket. Stealing another glance at Bobby and Jay, she smiled. She wasn't specifically out to find a father for Jay. No doubt, he'd be better off with a steady male influence in his life, and she couldn't deny that he'd blossomed these past couple of months with Bobby around all the time. Once or twice she'd worried about the effect on Jay should they break up. But it had seemed like borrowing tomorrow's troubles, and she'd focused instead on the happy interaction between the two who had taken so completely to each other.

She finished laying out their lunch and shifted her weight to ease the dull ache in her leg. Her heart swelled at the sight of her two men rolling and giggling. She hadn't pursued this relationship with Bobby because she was looking to provide a father for Jay. But she had to admit, he'd never been more attractive than he was right now, rolling around on a quilt her grandmother had made, having a tickle fest with her little boy.

"Lunch!" she called, before the joy and gratitude she felt had the opportunity to show itself in the form of tears. "Who's hungry?"

"Me, me, me!" The boys shouted in unison.

"How does peanut butter and jelly sound?"

"Mmm. I like peanut butter and jelly!" Jay stood up and began to hop around in his excitement.

"Sounds good to me, too." Bobby pushed himself up into a sitting position and reclined against a nearby tree.

"I guess y'all will have to fight for it then, because I only made one PB&J."

"Oh!" Bobby clutched his chest and made a pained

sound like he'd just been shot. "I guess he can have it."

"Smart move." She sat Jay down, put his sandwich on a paper plate in front of him, and handed him a sippy cup full of milk. "I've grown quite fond of you, Bobby. I'd hate to have to watch while Jay took you out over a peanut butter sandwich. He would, you know."

"I don't doubt it." Bobby stretched his legs out and took the plate she offered him.

Warmth spread as his steady gaze moved from her hands, up the length of one arm and to her face. He smiled when their gazes finally locked. It was like he could reach out and touch her physically with a simple glance. And she was having an increasingly difficult time keeping her thoughts pure where he was concerned.

As for Bobby, he was clearly a physical man. At first he hadn't wanted to touch her at all. He'd been afraid to. But once that ice had been broken, he touched her constantly. Whenever possible he held her hand, or draped an arm around her. He liked to hug, and he liked to kiss.

They'd agreed not to let things go further than that. But once or twice she'd been sorely tempted to throw caution, along with her moral convictions, to the wind. Watching him now where he leaned against a solid oak, looking out over the sprawling park, she was thankful that he was as committed to not crossing that line as she. He would be impossible to resist if he applied even the slightest pressure.

He turned, catching her staring at him, and heat rushed to her face. She bit her lower lip and looked down into her plate, suppressing an embarrassed grin.

"This is nice."

She managed a glance at him, prompted by the

warm, inviting tone of his voice.

"We never did anything like this when I was a kid."

She knit her brows together. "Never?"

He shook his head and took a sip of tea.

"We used to do this a lot. At least once a month in the spring and summer–as long as it wasn't too hot." She sipped her own tea and smiled reminiscently. "Sometimes we'd come to this very park and sit in this spot."

"And you and Caroline would fight over the peanut butter sandwich?"

Meagan smiled. "She knew better."

He nodded, something in his expression saying he didn't quite believe her.

"And you *never* went on a picnic when you were a kid?"

Again, he shook his head. "My dad was rarely sober enough to behave like a father. And my poor mother...she was just too beat down to take matters into her own hands."

Meagan swallowed and looked briefly at Jay, who ate his sandwich contentedly, paying them no attention. "Beat down? By your father?"

Bobby nodded. "By him, by life...mostly by him."

"And you? Did he beat you down, too?"

He gave a grunt that may have been meant as some kind of ironic laugh, but she wasn't sure about that. With a nod, he drifted off into his own world of memories. She watched his smile fade and the lines of his face harden, and she wished she knew what to do or say to bring him back, to make him forget all that and enjoy everything he had now.

She loved him, and she wanted to make him

happy.

Maybe expressing those feelings to him now would do the trick. He may not respond in kind. But regardless of how he reacted, that was how she felt. She wanted it to be out in the open.

"Bobby." Her voice was uncharacteristically soft and timid sounding. She chewed on her bottom lip and waited for him to answer.

Just as he looked up at her, Jay jumped up and ran off into the distance shouting something about a bird. Meagan looked in the direction he ran and saw a roadrunner darting back and forth, panicked at the sight of the charging child. Finally it gained enough momentum to take flight.

"Jay, come back!" Her call stopped him in his tracks and he turned around. A slow grin spread across his face. She could read his mind. He'd just realized that he had the immediate power to make them participate in a game of chase. An instant later, the chase was on.

She rose stiffly to retrieve him, but only stood, watching him for a second. Bobby came to stand beside her.

"He's not going to stop and come back, is he?"

Bobby shook his head. "I wouldn't."

She took a step, but he stopped her with a hand on her back.

"Audrey, honey, you just sit yourself back down. I'll go get him."

Meagan blinked a few times, too stunned to speak as Bobby trotted off after Jay, seeming not to realize he'd just called her by another woman's name.

The flickering light from the television cast mesmerizing shadows all around Meagan's living room. She watched them shift and change as her mind processed what had happened at the park just a few hours ago.

"Meagan?"

She started at the sound of her name, almost having to shake her head to clear it. She'd drifted off into her own world, and judging by the look on Bobby's face, he'd noticed. He'd probably asked her a question, and she hadn't even heard it.

"Everything OK?"

No! She wanted to say. *Everything is not OK. You called me by someone else's name earlier. And just who is Audrey, anyway?* She wanted to fly off the handle, and get irrational, and demand answers.

The fact was, however, that she knew exactly who Audrey was. Now that she had a name, she'd been turning it over and over in her mind all day, trying to imagine what she must look like, wondering if she regretted not having Bobby around anymore.

She looked up at him. "Everything's fine. I'm just kind of tired."

He nodded, apparently satisfied, and leaned back into the cushions, pulling her closer as he pointed the remote at the television in search of something to watch.

After he'd settled on a channel and become engrossed in the program she stole a glance at his profile.

Do you still love her? She wanted so much to ask. Her eyes stung with tears she struggled to hold back. *If you had the chance would you leave me and go back to her?*

"*Do you still love her?*"

"What?" Bobby sat up and hit the mute button.

It was all she could do to keep from clamping a hand over her mouth when she realized she'd whispered the question. She stammered a bit. "Um...uh...nothing. I was just...thinking. I guess I accidentally started thinking out loud."

"You asked if I still loved her."

Chilly air slid around her to fill the sudden void Bobby's arms left as he sat up straighter and turned to look at her.

"Is that why you've been zoning in and out all evening? You've been wondering if I'm still in love with my ex?"

Heat flooded her face, and she looked down in shame. She should be above it. She should be secure enough, confident enough not to worry about something like this. She was a grown woman with a child and a failed marriage of her own.

"What brought this up, Meagan?"

If she was going to mention it, now was the time. But she couldn't bring herself to do it. He hadn't called her Audrey on purpose. He didn't even realize he'd done it. And to point it out would only make him feel like a heel, which he wasn't. "I guess it was bound to come up eventually."

He sighed heavily and slid both his arms around her as he leaned back into the couch again. She wrapped both her arms around him and snuggled closely, burying her face in the front of his shirt.

"I'm sorry, Bobby," she murmured. "It doesn't matter. I shouldn't have asked."

She felt the gentle pressure of his finger under her chin, lifting her face to look at him.

"Do you still love *your* ex?" His voice was gentle.

He wasn't being competitive or cruel. He was making a point. But as much as she wanted to give him a resounding, undeniable 'no,' she couldn't. She wasn't *in love* with Kevin. But she'd spent a good chunk of her life with him and been happy. She had loved him that way once, and would never forget those feelings.

"I love *you*, Meagan." Tears welled in her eyes as he continued. "She threw me out. I didn't want to go, and I tried hard to convince her to take me back. Maybe some part of me will always love her. Just like some part of you will probably always love your ex-husband. She was a huge part of my life. But *this* is my life now."

She tightened her hold on him as her tears began to fall. "I love you, too, Bobby."

She felt his arms tighten around her as he pressed a kiss into her hair, then whispered, "Don't ever doubt it."

8

"OK! Everybody smile and wave!" Patrick pointed the camera at the festive group sitting at the table.

This was more than a little awkward, but Bobby smiled and waved anyway. He never looked like himself on video, and he certainly wouldn't look right in *this* video. He glanced at Meagan, who sat adjacent to him with Jay on her lap. They both smiled and waved at the camera, perfectly at ease. Meagan tried to keep Jay's pointed birthday hat securely on his head, but he wouldn't have it. No sooner did she push it into place than he pulled it off again and tossed it to the floor. Bobby grinned. Who could blame the kid? Those pointy little birthday hats always made him think of a dunce cap.

"Happy birthday to me!" Jay's ecstatic outburst elicited a cheer from the adults.

From behind him Bobby heard Mary Anne start singing "Happy Birthday". When she was about halfway through the song she set a rather lopsided, homemade cake on the kitchen table in front of Jay, who clapped and took a deep breath, awaiting his cue to blow out the three candles adorning the top.

Bobby sang along, his throat constricting as Mary Anne gave Jay a quick peck on the top of his head, touched Meagan lightly on the cheek, then moved around the table to stand behind him. He nearly started as her hands came to rest on his shoulders. His voice faltered nearly to a halt. But remembering the camera, he pushed his shock at her familial touch aside, smiling and clapping as the song ended and Jay blew out his candles.

The last family gathering Bobby had been at had been a birthday party for Audrey. Her family had met at the local diner because her parents wouldn't step foot in her house as long as he lived there. And he most definitely had not been welcome in their home. There had been few laughs and smiles that night, though he'd tried hard to please them all. Hard for him, at any rate. Which meant he stayed sober and didn't push or shove anyone.

Bobby glanced up and met Mary Anne's smiling gaze as she handed him his cake. He tried to swallow down the ache that had developed in his throat. He was welcome here. Maybe for the first time in his life, he was carving out his place in a normal family, and they approved of him.

"Bobby?"

The soft whisper drew his attention. He looked at Meagan, and she furrowed her brow at him, mouthing the words, "You OK?"

He cleared his throat, smiled and nodded.

Jay bounced up and down in Meagan's lap as he dug into his piece of cake, managing to cover half his face in chocolate frosting with the first bite.

"Here, Mom." Meagan backed her chair away from the table and stood, holding Jay by one arm around his waist. "Why don't you take over with chocolate boy here, and let me start clearing the dinner dishes."

"With pleasure!" Mary Anne swept Jay into her

arms and covered him with kisses. He giggled and twisted in her arms, reaching toward his cake. Meagan began gathering dishes as her mom sat down.

Bobby stood, picked up a few dishes, and followed her.

"Everything OK?" she asked quietly as they set the plates into the sink. "You looked a little freaked out for a second."

"Everything's perfect." When she turned to face him, he slid his arms around her waist and pulled her close, kissing her lightly. She laid one hand against his cheek and kissed him back.

"I'm so glad you decided to come. Especially since Caroline couldn't make it."

"I'm glad I did, too. I almost didn't. You made it sound like birthday parties are a sacred family tradition. I didn't want to intrude. But...well, how often does a boy turn three?"

"Unhand my daughter!" Bobby started at Patrick's booming voice. Instinctively, guiltily, he turned Meagan loose and stepped back a pace before realizing her father was teasing him. "What will the boy think?"

"Oh, Daddy, quit your teasing." Meagan grinned at her father. "Currently, the boy is only thinking about how he can persuade Grandma to give him another piece of cake."

Patrick crossed to them and clapped a friendly hand on Bobby's shoulder. He almost winced. He didn't know why. He'd come with no expectations as to how the evening would turn out. By his standards, this was about as well as it could possibly go. But he couldn't shake a nagging, indefinable feeling that had him wanting to look over his shoulder, to make absolutely certain that everything really was as good as it seemed.

The phone rang and Meagan reached for the cordless phone on the counter. Bobby heard the muffled sound of a male voice, and her smile vanished. She folded one arm across her chest and looked down, remaining silent for a long moment. The voice spoke again.

"Yes, I'm here," she said at length.

Patrick and Mary Anne both fell silent and turned their full attention to their daughter. The mood of the room turned somber. Only Jay continued eating his cake and chatting happily, totally unaware of the changed atmosphere.

"What do you want?" Meagan glanced at her boy, and Bobby knew who was calling. "If you want to do something nice for him, then why don't you send a check? Oh, I don't know, Kevin, for child support maybe? To help pay off the debt collectors who won't stop calling *me* to settle the bills *you* filed bankruptcy on?"

Bobby knew she harbored no tender feelings for her ex-husband at the moment. If the hostile tone of her voice was any indication, she'd sooner see Kevin strung up in the town square than let him back into her heart. Still, his jaw set, seemingly against his will, and a hot, ember-like feeling settled in his chest. He loved her, and she loved him. Now her ex spoke with her concerning intimate family matters, intruding on what he was beginning to think of as *his* family, and ruining the perfect evening they'd been having. Jealousy flared, red hot, and spread like fire through him.

"How could you not know, Kevin?" The hostility in her voice gave way suddenly to weary frustration. "We opened those accounts together. They're not going to take my name off of what's left of them just because a judge said 'here you take these.'"

Her shoulders sagged, and she made a half turn away from everyone else, as if suddenly deciding this was a private conversation. Bobby's heart started to pound with the rush of adrenaline that anger always caused in him. In considering whether or not to act upon the urge to snatch the phone away from her and inform Kevin of his presence and intentions, he realized that, at some point, he'd balled his hands into fists at his sides.

"What can you do about it?" Her voice softened in a way he didn't like, as if she was about to forgive him. "It's done... Yes, I understand that you never intended for any of that to affect us, but it does. And I can't afford to pay these bills."

The sudden, almost overwhelming impulse to take the phone from her and hurl it across the room mingled with a vision of him grabbing her by the shoulders, his fingers digging into her flesh as he shook her until she swore never to take a call from Kevin again. The muscle in his jaw worked fiercely as he gritted his teeth. A deep breath did little to help him control the rising fury. Still, he took another, and another. He had to get out of this room before he said or did something he'd regret.

All eyes were on him as he fled. Trying to keep his pace normal, he passed through the kitchen, then the living room, and into the bathroom, where he quietly shut the door.

Bobby unclenched his fists and laid both trembling hands on the counter, then looked at his angry reflection in the mirror.

"Lord, help me control this." One deep breath,

then another. "Help me control this."

He had no idea how long he stood there, staring in the mirror, uttering the same prayer over and over. But finally a knock on the door startled him. He stood up straight and rubbed the back of his neck, breathing deeply for a moment.

He gripped the doorknob for a long second, took a breath, then pulled the door open. Meagan stood in the hall. The concern etched into her features pierced his heart.

"Bobby, I'm sorry–"

"Don't apologize." He shook his head and stepped out into the hall.

"He called to wish Jay a happy birthday. He's never done that before. I...I shouldn't have..."

"Meagan, he's your ex-husband, Jay's father. He's part of your life whether I like it or not. *I'm* sorry. I overreacted." He reached for her hand, and she intertwined her fingers with his.

"I was just afraid that if–"

He cut her off with a groan as he pulled her into his arms. "Meagan, the very last thing I ever want you to be is afraid. OK? I don't ever want you to be afraid to tell me something, or ask about something, or..." He looked into her eyes, raised an open palm to lay aside her cheek, and tenderly touched the first woman in his life who knew him and didn't flinch when he raised his hand. "I'm amazed that you love me." His voice was little more than a whisper.

Her expression relaxed, and she smiled softly.

He pulled her into his arms and took a long, deep breath. She wasn't afraid of him, although she had good reason to be. No. He was the scared one. Terrified. Of doing something to lose her. Or worse, of hurting her.

Sober, he'd never behaved aggressively toward anyone. But tonight he'd wanted to. He'd wanted to have extreme words with Kevin Layne, but had been tempted to act against the one who was available instead–the one he loved most.

If he ever lashed out at her in his anger, he didn't know how he'd live with himself.

కోల

Meagan stole a glance at her watch and sighed softly. Mrs. Clarkson had been filling Meagan in on the details of her upcoming family reunion for most of the past forty-five minutes. She lifted a tress of the elderly woman's white hair and gently teased it.

Suddenly, seemingly from nowhere, the woman laughed. Meagan blinked and tried to shake the romantic fog from her head. Good thing there wouldn't be a quiz on the reunion preparations, because she probably hadn't heard half of what Mrs. Clarkson said.

"Meagan?" Mrs. Clarkson's laughter stopped as abruptly as it had begun. The now hushed, suspicious tone of the woman's voice drew Meagan's attention.

"Hmm?"

"I don't mean to alarm you, dear. But there's a young man standing by the counter. He's been staring at you since he got here."

She grinned and glanced over to see Bobby leaning against the counter, watching her intently. She'd been so preoccupied with thoughts of him that she hadn't heard the bell on the front door, or even noticed him standing there, ten feet away. Heat rushed to her face and her smile widened.

"That's my boyfriend." Meagan matched Mrs. Clarkson's conspiratorial tone.

"Oh, I see. I didn't know you had a *boyfriend*."

Don't sound so shocked! Meagan suppressed a giggle at Mrs. Clarkson's bemused tone as she put the finishing touches on the hairdo and sprayed it liberally before removing the cape. It was all she could do to keep from drumming fingers on the counter and tapping her foot while Mrs. Clarkson dug through her purse in search of payment.

"Thank you, Mrs. Clarkson." She took the check with a smile when the older woman finally offered it.

"Thank you, dear." Mrs. Clarkson moved gracefully past Bobby and out the front door.

Finally, she was free.

"So what were you thinking about while you weren't paying attention to your customer?"

She sighed and affected her most bored expression. "The laundry."

Bobby gasped and took a step back, raising one hand to his chest. He kept the other hand fully behind his back. She peeked around, trying to see what he had hidden.

"Since you're so busy," he drawled, pulling a colorful bouquet from behind his back, "I guess you couldn't possibly find time to put these in some water."

She beamed as she took the flowers from him. "I guess I could make time."

"Good." He leaned across the counter and kissed her lightly. "Now, how about lunch?"

"I'll be right back." She turned to head to the back room, but didn't get halfway before Alicia stepped into her path, taking the flowers from her and inhaling their fragrance with a smile.

"I'll take care of these for you. You go on."

"Thanks, Alicia." Meagan found her purse, then joined Bobby.

Outside, the sun felt glorious and warm. She closed her eyes and turned her face up, feeling as if her skin were beginning to thaw. When Bobby took her hand in his, well, that just warmed her more.

Once a week or so, he took her to lunch at a little diner just a couple of blocks down the street from the salon, and they automatically headed in that direction. She smiled. They had formed a habit together. Neither one asked 'where to?' today. They both just assumed the same thing about their destination.

The high-pitched, electronic sound of Bobby's cell phone pierced the pleasant afternoon atmosphere, but he didn't miss a step beside her as he unfastened it from his belt and answered.

He stopped abruptly and turned her hand loose, pressing the phone close to one ear and trying to close off the street noise with the other.

"Mom?"

Meagan spun to face him. Only once since she'd met him had he spoken of his mother, and as far as she knew, he never talked to her.

"Slow down, Mom. What happened?"

He stood listening, as if he feared he might miss something crucial. Then he let out a deep breath that she hadn't even noticed he'd been holding. His shoulders sagged, and he groaned as he released his clamped ear and dragged the back of his hand across his mouth.

"When?"

She couldn't guess the news by his expression, other than the vague certainty that it was bad. In his eyes she saw an odd combination of sorrow and anger, maybe even relief.

"Yes, Mom, I'll come." He glanced apologetically at her before he continued. "I'll call you later when I know what my exact plans are. OK, bye."

He ended the call, then clipped the phone back in place.

His silence worried her. She laid a gentle hand on his arm.

"Bobby?"

His desperate expression made her heart constrict. "My father's dead."

❧❦

"I'm going with you."

"No." Bobby added a sternness to his voice that he knew wouldn't help the situation. "No. You're not going with me. Where I grew up is the last place I want to take you. Besides, what about Jay?"

"I've already talked with my mother. She has some vacation days she needs to use up before the summer's over. She wants to keep him."

"No." Even he noticed the lack of conviction in his voice now. "I can't take you there, Meagan. I just can't."

He dropped heavily down onto the couch. For her sake, he couldn't take her home for his father's funeral, although for his sake, he wanted to desperately. If she went along, it wouldn't matter what anyone else said, or did, or thought. She would be there next to him, reminding him, serving as living proof that he had changed. He was not the same man everyone there remembered.

She sat down and he reached for her hand. "Believe me, it's not that I don't want you with me, baby. I just don't want you to see all that."

"I know," she said softly. "And I don't particularly want to see it, either. I want to be with *you*. And, I realize the situation might not be ideal, but I would like to meet your family."

He shook his head and pushed to his feet, irritated that she was being so insistent. His family was precisely what he didn't want her to see.

"You haven't even told me the details, Bobby. How did he die? When? What happened?"

He expelled a long breath and crossed to the picture window that overlooked the back yard. The dusky light highlighted and shadowed Jay's tricycle, and the patio furniture. Out in the grass was a big, red ball, and a toddler-sized baseball bat. A swing hung from an old oak tree, making the perfect picture of all the little things that made a house a home. Things his father never provided.

"He had a massive heart attack. Mom said he went fast. Didn't know what hit him."

Too quick and easy for a man like him.

"It happened this morning. She handed him coffee as he sat down to watch T.V. When she came back through the room ten minutes later, he was already gone."

"Oh, Bobby." He heard her rise, and felt her warmth a second later. "I'm sorry."

"Don't be." He regretted the bitter, angry sorrow he heard in his own voice. He didn't want her to see this side of him. But he couldn't stop the thought once it started. *I'm not.*

"How do you feel?"

He could feel her steady gaze as she reached and linked fingers with his own. He shrugged. "I don't know. I should feel sad, right? I should feel grief that he's gone." He swallowed and cleared his throat, trying to tamp down the ache beginning there. "If anything, I feel guilty."

"Guilty? What could you possibly have to feel guilty for where he's concerned?"

He shook his head. "I don't know. I can't explain it. Maybe because I got away from him. At least, I thought I did. I'm trying to. I left him behind without a thought that maybe I could say or do something to help him change."

A small cough emanated from the baby monitor on the end table across the room, and Bobby turned his head to listen more closely. Jay settled back down, muttering something in a sleepy haze.

"I should have told him about my faith." Bobby cast a sideways glance at her. "I hadn't spoken with him in four or five years. Every so often I'll talk to my mother, but not him. I never even told him I'd become a Christian. I left town without even saying goodbye."

"There's no way you could have known he would die now."

"I should have at least said goodbye. I should have gone to him and tried to convince him, for my mother's sake." He reached up and pinched the bridge of his nose, as if that could stop this flow of emotion. "I guess she's free now."

"Oh, Bobby," she whispered.

The catch in her voice drew his attention, and he turned to find her in tears.

"Don't cry, baby." He pulled her close, pressing a kiss into her hair. "Don't cry for him. You didn't even know him."

"I'm not crying for him." Her words were muffled by the fierceness of her embrace. "Please take me with you. I love you, and I want to be there for you. You want me there, too. I know you do."

He sighed wearily. She was right. If she wanted to go as badly as he wanted her to, there was no good reason for her to stay behind. She'd already made arrangements for Jay. She probably already had her suitcase packed. Wanting to go with him was her nature. It was how she was raised. Her family came together in a crisis, they supported each other, and that's what she wanted to do for him. And he needed that.

"OK." He nodded and looked into her eyes. "Can we leave by noon tomorrow?"

Relief lit her smile. She nodded. "I'll cancel my appointments."

9

"Here it is." Bobby's voice drew Meagan's attention from the scenery outside the passenger side window. She turned in time to see him take a deep breath. "Blithe Settlement, Texas. Look there! That's new." He pointed to a chain sub sandwich shop. "Must be movin' up in the world."

She smiled and slid her hand across the center console to touch his arm. However mixed his feelings might be about the circumstances that brought them here today, he was coming home. His excitement might not be bubbling over, but it was there.

"You hungry?"

Meagan pressed a hand to her stomach and tried, unsuccessfully, to stifle a yawn. She stretched her arms and legs. "Mmm. I could eat a little something."

"Does a burger sound OK?"

"Sounds good." She focused her attention, once again, on the scenery outside.

So, this was where he grew up: This little town beside the highway, a collection of old, falling-down houses and abandoned buildings. Up ahead, weeds had begun to overtake an old, closed-down gas station situated directly across the highway from a newer convenience store. The new one looked all right, but next to it was an old, rusting metal building, a part completely overtaken by some kind of wide-leafed vine. A few houses stood sprinkled in among the businesses along the highway, and right behind them, not a hundred yards from their back doors, ran the railroad tracks.

"The train must be deafening for the people who live in those houses." Meagan stiffened–she hadn't meant to say that out loud. She bit her lip and glanced at Bobby. "I mean, I probably wouldn't be able to sleep."

"You get to where you don't even hear it."

"You lived that close to the tracks?"

"Yeah." He glanced at her quickly, wearing a half grin. "But on the other side."

"Oh, please!" She groaned and rolled her eyes at the joke. But there was nothing funny about the town.

Under other circumstances, she probably would have wrinkled her nose and refused to stop here no matter how urgent the need. It was small, old, and so far, it looked junky. But this was the place Bobby called home, the place he ran away from. Knowing *that* probably colored her judgment regarding Blithe Settlement. Lubbock had its junky sections, too. Every town did. She took a deep breath and decided to give this little town the benefit of the doubt for now. It was his hometown. And she could tell from the absent half smile on his face, that his time here hadn't been all bad.

What are you thinking about right now? The question died on her tongue for fear it was Audrey who occupied the thoughts that made him smile so fondly.

He turned onto Main Street and drove a few more blocks until they came to a little diner. At first she only grinned at the sight of the weathered, old sign with the name of the restaurant hand painted in bold black letters. But the grin soon turned into a giggle.

"The Prickly Pear?" She glanced at him quickly, then back to the building. "Is that really what it's called?"

"Sure that's what it's called." He sounded bewildered by her amusement.

"Do they actually serve prickly pear here?"

"Well, no. But you can't get a better burger anywhere."

She burst out laughing. "Could that be because there's no other place in this town to get a burger?"

He grinned. "I told you it was a small town."

"Oh, I'm just teasing. Isn't your mom expecting us?"

He shook his head. "I told her I didn't know what time we'd get into town and that we'd eat before we got there. She's not expecting to have to feed us."

Meagan nodded as he pulled into a space and parked, but the idea was foreign to her. Her folks wouldn't hear of her not having dinner with them if she'd just gotten back into town after a lengthy absence. They'd wait on her until midnight if they had to. But this was his trip home. She wouldn't question his need to do it his way.

He came around the truck and opened the door for her. She took his hand and slid out. His fingers tightened around hers.

"I'm glad you're here." His voice was warm and soft. It gave her butterflies.

She smiled, wishing suddenly that he'd pull her into his arms and kiss her for all he was worth. Judging by the glint in his eyes, he too, was giving the possibility some thought. Wouldn't *that* give the folks around here something to talk about?

A passing truck backfired. Bobby cleared his

throat and stepped back. His fingers tightened around her hand as he pulled her to his side. A few steps had them at the front door. He pulled it open for her, and she stepped inside. A wiry, middle-aged man sat behind the front counter reading a newspaper. At the sound of the bell on the door he looked up and gave her a kindly smile, but the expression froze on his face when he looked over her shoulder. The man's gaze slid back to her as his smile faded.

It was seven o'clock on a weeknight, and the diner wasn't crowded. But several booths and tables were occupied, and several conversations came to an abrupt halt as Bobby stepped up beside her. Without looking, she reached for his hand, feeling a little less apprehensive when his fingers closed around hers. He'd told her how he expected folks to react to his return. But these people weren't staring at him. They were staring at her—and not subtly, either.

He let her hand go and moved a little closer, and she felt the comforting pressure of his hand at the small of her back as he ushered her past the cash register to a corner booth.

"Wade." He greeted the man behind the counter curtly as they passed.

"Bobby."

Meagan could feel the man's stare follow them across the room. Heat rushed to her face under his intense scrutiny as well as that of the diner's other occupants. The noise level picked up again, though the voices didn't sound as candid as before. A quick glance around the room confirmed her assumption that most conversations had turned to them. In a far corner a woman was leaning in close to her companion, talking softly into his ear and casting occasional covert glances their way.

"Hi, Bobby."

Meagan looked up at the waitress who greeted him, and the only person in the room who appeared to harbor any affection for him at all.

"I heard about your dad." She reached out and laid a hand on his shoulder, her small town twang softening in the compassionate way of a woman more than willing to offer comfort. "I'm sorry."

He nodded. "Thanks."

The waitress looked from Bobby to her.

"Jenny, this is Meagan Layne." He reached across the table for her hand. "Meagan, this is Jenny Lawson. We went to school together."

"It's good to meet you." Jenny turned her attention back to him. "You just in town for the funeral, or are you planning on stayin' for awhile?"

"Just for the funeral."

"Where you livin' now?"

"Lubbock."

Jenny nodded, seemingly a little put off, Meagan could only assume, by his lack of enthusiasm. The thought gave her a small measure of comfort. "Well, what can I get y'all to drink?" A group from a table across the room got up to leave, filing toward the cash register, all casting glances their way. One smiled awkwardly and waved when Bobby looked up and gave a nod.

No one here wanted to have anything to do with him. Except for the waitress, who hovered around their table too much, laughing and joking with him, while totally ignoring her. No one else came over to say hello, or ask what he'd been doing the past couple of years. All they did was stare—at him and at the new woman he'd brought.

"Here you go." Jenny set their burgers on the table and cast a pointed glance at her. "No pickles. Just the way you like it, Bobby."

He smiled a soft, genuine smile. "Thanks, Jenny."

Meagan unfolded her paper napkin and spread it across her lap.

So Jenny knew him. There may have even been some kind of relationship between them. She resisted the urge to say anything about it as she watched the waitress stroll back to the counter. *He's here with me.* The thought gave her less and less comfort.

The bell on the front door announced the arrival of another couple of customers. Their interest turned to the corner booth after a cursory survey of the room. She glanced back at Bobby, who sat stoically, silently, salting his fries, either not noticing or not caring.

In the past few months he had become a part of her family. Her parents already thought of him as a son-in-law, and her own thoughts drifted down that same track constantly. But here was this whole part of his life that she knew nothing about. This town, his family, his old friends and enemies...suddenly it felt as if she didn't know him at all.

క∞

Belligerence was beginning to swell up in his gut like an ominous thunderhead. Bobby hadn't been back in town two hours yet, and he could feel the old attitude boiling back to the surface. Anger surged every time someone did a double take when they noticed him, and then turned to whisper to a companion, or worse, quickly turned away, careful not make eye contact, pretending not to see him at all.

Meagan sensed the difference in him, too. He could tell she did. She'd grown quiet, timid. Almost like she didn't know him anymore. Almost like she was afraid of him. That just made it worse.

And now, as he drove down his old street, the realization hit him that she was about to see the place and the people he grew up with. He turned into the driveway and turned the engine off.

It hadn't changed one bit. It was a little, old house, in the old part of town, white siding with peeling paint, two beat-up, broken down pickup trucks on cinderblocks in the side yard, overgrown with weeds and buffalo grass. Worn out toys, which had belonged to him and his brother and sisters, now well-used by his nieces and nephews, littered the front yard and old concrete porch.

Bobby's grip on the steering wheel tightened. At least he wouldn't have to introduce her to his father.

He almost started at the sudden feel of her hand on his arm. Taking a deep, stabilizing breath, he turned to her and forced a smile.

"I love you." Her soft, sweet words soothed his nerves. What he had with her was the closest thing to normal he'd ever had. Not long ago, he would have said that Audrey was the best thing that ever happened to him, and up until he'd met Meagan, that had been true. But this was even better. He hadn't spoiled it yet.

The old screen door on his mom's front door swung open and Tommy stepped out, beer in hand, to wait for them to get out. Bobby's parents had four kids, none of whom turned out all that great. But Tommy was the worst of the bunch. If Bobby's behavior toward women had been deplorable, Tommy's was downright heinous. Bobby didn't want Meagan anywhere near him, and he sure didn't intend to leave him alone with her for any amount of time.

He cast a quick glance to find her watching Tommy closely. Maybe he should warn her. Tell her just to keep her distance as best she could. She was perceptive and smart. Maybe she'd size Tommy up on her own. The expression on her face said she'd already formed an accurate opinion. When she turned to him, her brow furrowed with worry, he tried to smile reassuringly.

"That's my brother, Tommy."

She nodded and looked back to where Tommy had leaned one shoulder up against a porch column. He took a long, slow sip from the can in his hand. The grin he shot at them looked almost sinister.

"Just try to stay away from him, OK? Stay with me or Mom or my sisters."

She nodded again and turned back to him, her eyes wide and nervous. He'd frightened her.

No. He hadn't spoiled what he had with her yet. But this trip home probably would.

❧❦

Appalled might not be just the right word to describe Meagan's initial reaction to Bobby's childhood home. But it came close. The house itself probably wasn't any older than the one she lived in now. But it looked...she hated to even consider the term with regard to anything related to the man she loved. But it looked trashy. Stereotypically trashy. And Tommy coming out onto the porch in his old, frayed t-shirt, jeans, and beat up boots, with a two-day-old beard, holding onto a beer, and leering at her before she even got out of the truck put just the right finishing touch on the whole picture.

Bobby opened her door and she stepped out into a totally unfamiliar world.

Tommy slowly looked her up and down, letting his gaze wander wherever it wanted to. Making a point of it, in fact. Determined not to let him see how nervous he made her, she defiantly met his gaze when he managed to return it to her face.

He answered her with a smile so like Bobby's that she would have called him handsome under other circumstances. But where Bobby's heart and mind were clean, Tommy's were corrupt. He exuded filth.

Thankfully, Bobby stepped in between them and led the way up the front porch steps.

"That's some girl you got there, Bobby. You gonna introduce us?" The lewd emphasis he'd placed on the words "some girl" made her skin crawl.

Bobby stopped at the top of the steps and paused for a moment that lasted way too long while his jaw muscles worked hard. She thought for a moment that Bobby might punch his brother, or maybe his brother would punch him. Silent tension charged the air as the two assessed each other and the situation, as if to determine who would make the first move and why. Finally, Bobby took a deep breath.

"Tommy, this is Meagan Layne. Meagan, this is my...brother, Tommy."

That was it. No handshake, no greeting, no acknowledgment of their father's death, no pleasantries. Just two brothers who seemed to hate each other. One declared silently that this was his territory, and anything in it was fair game. The other promised to be here no longer than absolutely necessary.

Bobby pulled the screen door, then pushed open the front door, letting her inside.

The living room was tidier than she expected, based on the condition of the yard. Its furnishings weren't new, but they were neat and clean. A photograph on a bookcase to her right caught her attention, and she stopped to examine it.

"That's me." Bobby pointed to a sweet-faced little kid in a thirty or so year old family portrait. "There's Tommy. He's the oldest, then Nicole, then me, then Hope. Then there's my mother and my father."

Meagan looked back at the photo, hardly able to believe the two good looking parents and four gorgeous children really had lived in the midst of the turmoil that Bobby had alluded to. They looked so normal. So happy. She leaned in to take a closer look at his father. "I bet it doesn't even feel like he's gone yet."

"Oh, he's gone all right."

She started and turned. She hadn't heard Tommy come back inside. But now his voice filled the room in the manner of a man whose sense of decorum has been impaired by at least one beer too many.

"I know he's gone because otherwise he'd be sitting right there in that chair drinking beer and watching T.V. Never did much else, except maybe slap his family around." Tommy paused, narrowed his eyes and leered. "Course, you probably already know some about that, don't you, darlin'. Oh, wait. I remember now. My little brother went and got himself saved, didn't he? Got some religion. That's right, he's good now."

The pressure of Bobby's hand on her back urged her onward through the house to the kitchen. It was a big, open room with a large, rectangular, oak table in the center. Bobby's mother sat at one end cradling a glass of iced tea in both hands. She looked up when they entered.

"Bobby, baby!" She rose and rushed to put her arms around him, tears pooling in her eyes. When she spoke again her voice was muffled against the front of his shirt. "You're here. I'm so glad you're here."

"Well, don't *you* look good." One of the other two women at the table spoke up, causing his mom to take a step back. She looked him up and down with a sniff, dabbing at her eyes with her fingers tips.

"Oh, honey, you do! You look so good. Life in Lubbock must be treating you well." Her attention turned to Meagan. "And who's this you brought with you?"

He reached for her hand. "Mom, this is Meagan Layne. Meagan, this is my mom, Karen Kerr."

Meagan extended her hand to the other woman who took it warmly. "It's so good to meet you. Thank you for coming. Can I get you something to drink?"

She was about to nod and say how much she'd love a glass of tea, but Bobby interrupted.

"We're not staying long. We had a long drive, and I'd like to get Meagan to the Thomasons' so she can get some rest. I just wanted her to meet you tonight."

"Oh, OK." Karen didn't try to mask her disappointment, nor did she protest.

"Meagan, this is my sister, Nicole."

The woman who had spoken sat, leaning casually back in her chair, scrutinizing her with narrowed eyes. "Pleased to meet you."

"And this is Laurel, Tommy's wife." Bobby introduced a petite, dark-haired woman at the other end of the table.

"Hi, Meagan."

"Mama, Mama!" A boy of about eight or nine bounded through the back door and into the kitchen, landing beside Laurel. "Can T.J. and me go down to the railroad tracks?"

"No."

"Please, Mama, just for a little while."

"No. Now it's getting dark outside, and we need to be heading home soon."

The kid's shoulders sagged, and he heaved a dramatic, defeated sigh. "Just for a minute? Just till it's time to go? I promise I'll come right when you call me."

"We should be going ourselves, Mama."

Meagan turned back to Bobby who had taken his mother into another embrace.

"I'll be back in awhile, but I want to get Meagan situated at Brent's house."

"Well, honey, she could stay here."

"They've already offered. They're expecting us. I'll be back."

Meagan blinked, overwhelmed.

Bobby turned to go, as did Meagan, and she almost ran right into Tommy, who made no effort to move. She swallowed. "Excuse me."

He stepped aside, but said nothing.

"It was nice to meet you all." She uttered her farewell softly. Then she turned to follow Bobby to the front door.

What she wanted to do was run.

∻∻

"I can stay in a motel."

Bobby closed the passenger door after Meagan got out. "Trust me on this one. You don't want to stay at the Four Star Motel."

"I don't know about this. I could stay at your mom's house."

"Absolutely not." He reached into the bed of the truck and hauled her small suitcase over the side. "You'll like the Thomasons. They're normal. Brent's a good friend to me–about the only one I have around here. I'll feel better with you here."

Meagan nodded. She didn't know about the local motel, but she definitely didn't want to stay at his mother's house. She also didn't know that staying with completely unrelated strangers was a preferable solution. "I don't want to impose..."

"You're not." Bobby put her suitcase down and took both her hands in his as she leaned back against his pickup. "When Brent heard about my dad, he called and asked if there was anything they could do. They want to help. They have this big old house, all to themselves. At least for now. It's the best place for you while you're here."

"OK. If you think so." She nodded and gave his hands a squeeze. She had no idea what to expect when she walked into this house. Since they'd arrived in this town she'd felt stuck in the *Twilight Zone*. But she put on her most confident expression. "What about you? Are you OK?"

"I'm good." He looked down at her hands. "I'm a lot better than I would be if you hadn't come along. I...I'm sorry about my brother."

"Don't apologize." The first signs of stubble were beginning to show on his face. She raised one hand and traced his stubbly jaw line with her finger. It made him look rougher than normal. More like Tommy. Still, she couldn't fathom how two brothers raised in the same home had turned out so completely different. *God's grace.* That was the only possible way. "You can't control how he behaves."

He nodded and glanced at her. "I know. I just..." He paused. His gaze searched hers for a long moment, during which the breath caught in her throat. Just like it always did when she knew he was about to kiss her. He dropped his gaze to her mouth just a second before he covered it with his.

Only on the hottest, stillest summer days did she ever notice the sound of cicadas while the sun was out. But after dark was another story. As a child she'd found comfort in their nightly concert, lying on her back, stargazing next to her little sister, in the cool St. Augustine grass of their backyard. That same feeling of comfort, of rightness, saturated her heart at this moment, and the sounds of the cicadas and crickets had fierce competition with the heartbeat pounding in her ears. The soft feel of Bobby's warm mouth on hers made her dizzy. She clung to him, wrapping her arms around his neck, pulling him closer and closer, until she was certain she could feel his heart beating as well. Her every muscle tensed with sensation as one of his hands slid slowly around her waist. He cradled her head with the other, his fingers winding their way into her hair as he pressed soft, slow kisses to her mouth, along her jaw, just beneath her earlobe.

"Oh, Bobby," she whispered hoarsely, as he pressed another to her throat. "I love you. I wish I could stay with you tonight."

"Me too, baby." Those words, spoken softly in her ear, acted like kerosene on a hot fire. But apparently he was under complete control. With one last gentle kiss, he smiled, pushing a few wayward strands of hair behind her ear. "But I've already made the arrangements, and they are not for us to stay at the same place tonight."

Smart move. She sighed and reached up to him for one last kiss.

"Come on. Let's go." Grabbing her suitcase in one hand and her hand with the other, he led her up the front porch steps to a cozy farm house. He knocked.

A pretty, blonde woman with big, round, blue eyes opened the door. She shot a cursory glance at him, but then her gazed fixed on Meagan curiously.

"Hi, Bobby." She rubbed her back and stretched, which emphasized the fact that she must be nearing the end of her third trimester. "Y'all come on in."

"Bobby!" A man, probably around Meagan's age, got off the sofa and crossed the homey living room to shake his hand enthusiastically. "It's good to see you, man. How've you been?"

"Good." Bobby nodded. "Really good, all things considered. I'd like y'all to meet Meagan Layne."

His friend smiled, green eyes lighting mischievously. "So *this* is Meagan. I've heard a lot about you. You know, Bobby here said you were pretty, but I don't think he did you justice."

Warmth spread through Meagan, making its way finally to her face. She had to look down for a moment or she feared she'd turn giddy. *He'd told his friends about her.*

"Meagan, this is Brent Thomason."

She reached out to shake his hand with a smile, thankful that Bobby had chosen this place for her to spend the couple of days she'd be here. These folks were normal. They were nice. She'd be comfortable here. Bobby put an arm around her shoulders and pulled her closer, directing her attention to Brent's wife.

"And this is Audrey."

10

Why would he bring her here?

Meagan pressed her flattened palm to her stomach in response to a sudden wave of nausea. Of all the places in this trashy little town... She'd be better off at the Four Star Motel, no matter what kind of stains covered the mattress. The feel of Bobby's kisses still lingered, warm on her mouth and neck, but this turn of events stunned her every bit as much as a good dousing with a bucket of cold water. Why on earth would he bring her *here*?

Vaguely aware that the conversation had gone on around her, she tried to pull herself back together. His point couldn't possibly have been to hurt her, he wasn't even aware that she knew who Audrey was. But the way Bobby looked at Audrey now made her want to cry.

"So, how was your drive?" Audrey asked, and Meagan tore her gaze away from the hunger she saw in Bobby's expression to look at the soft spoken, pregnant woman who stood there ruining everything.

"Um...fine." She swallowed and cleared her aching throat. "Longer than I thought it'd be."

"Can I get you something to drink?"

Bobby shook his head. "Nothing for me. I really should be getting back to my mother's."

"Meagan?"

"Could I get a glass of water?"

"Sure." Audrey nodded and turned toward the kitchen.

The feel of Bobby's hand at the small of her back almost made her jump. She turned to look at him.

"I'm gonna head on back now. I need to make sure that Mom's holding up OK."

She nodded. "OK."

"You'll be all right here?"

Meagan studied his features for a long moment. *Why would I be all right here?* The words almost tumbled out despite her effort to hold them back. But hold them back she did. Finally, she nodded.

"The funeral's at eleven, but I'll be by to pick you up around ten."

She nodded again and closed her eyes against the shivers that worked their way down her spine at the feel of his soft kiss on her cheek.

"Night," he said softly.

"Good night."

She saw the question flicker briefly across his face. *Is everything OK?*

But what could she say? This wasn't the time, and it certainly wasn't the place to start that conversation. It would have to wait.

"I'll walk you out." Brent's voice reminded her that they weren't alone enough to have a personal conversation, anyway, and the two men turned to walk outside as Audrey returned with her water.

"Thanks." Meagan took the glass and sipped slowly, stealing a glance at the other woman over the rim.

Soft was the best word to describe her. She had soft blonde hair, a round face with soft blue eyes. A petite woman, she was at least six inches shorter than Meagan, maybe more. Even so late in her pregnancy, Audrey was small, well-proportioned, and exceedingly feminine. Meagan had never been ashamed of her height, but next to Bobby's ex, she felt awkward and gangly.

"Would you like to sit down?"

She nodded and perched on the very edge of the sofa. "Thank you so much for letting me stay here."

Audrey smiled, seemingly relieved that she had finally said something. "Well, we couldn't have you staying at the Four Star Motel. No self-respecting citizen of Blithe Settlement would let something like that happen. And Bobby's family...well, they're not any better."

She glanced at Audrey who returned a level, knowing stare.

"You know, don't you?"

Meagan nodded. There was no point in pretending now.

"When I heard about you, I wondered if he'd tell you about me."

"No. He would never..." She let her voice trail off. He hadn't told her specific details, but that didn't mean he never would. She cast a glance down at her knees. After the funeral, maybe on the long drive home, she'd make him give her a more thorough account of his past. "He's told me very little about you. And he's never mentioned you by name. Not on purpose. He accidentally called me by your name once. That's how I know who you are."

"Oh." Audrey looked down.

"He didn't even realize he did it. And I never said anything about it."

"So he doesn't realize that you know who I am."

Meagan shook her head. "I can't imagine he would have brought me here if he did."

"No. Me either."

They fell into a silence made even more awkward by the knowledge they shared. Bobby must have still been talking to Brent. They were good friends...*probably the best one I have in this town...*

Although how that happened, given the fact that Brent was married to Bobby's ex-girlfriend, she couldn't begin to fathom. Before now, his past had been something vague and indistinct, as if he were talking about someone else whenever the subject came up. But now, face to face with the woman who had suffered most at his hands, what had only been briefly spoken of became a hard reality.

"So. You're from Lubbock?" Audrey tilted her head, which called attention to a small, jagged scar high up on her left cheekbone, just in front of her ear.

Meagan blinked and looked away. "Um...yes." She glanced at the scar again. Had Bobby put it there? She shook her head, dismissing the thought. "Have you ever been?"

Audrey shook her head. "I've never been further west than Abilene."

Meagan nodded and sighed. "I'm sorry, Audrey. Please don't think me rude. But I have to...it's just that...well, Bobby hasn't told me a great deal about his relationship with you. But if what he *has* told me is true, I can't believe you'd be too eager to have him, or his new girlfriend around. And I can't believe that your husband would allow it. And yet they're outside now...and Bobby said that you and Brent were probably the only friends he had here...and you should have seen how people reacted to him when we stopped for supper...it's like a different world." She let her voice trail off as she looked at the glass of water in her hands. She didn't venture another look at Audrey, but could feel her steady gaze just the same. She sipped as the silence grew more and more disconcerting.

"It is a little strange, isn't it?" Audrey's tone was compassionate and maybe even a little self-deprecating.

The tension released itself finally in a nervous laugh. "Just a little."

Audrey laughed, nodded, and finally sighed. "Oh, where to start...Bobby's told you quite a bit about himself?"

Meagan relaxed a little and nodded. "He's been a Christian for a couple of years. He's a recovering alcoholic. He was abused as a child. He used to...um..."

"Abuse me." Audrey added frankly. "We don't need to euphemize it."

Meagan nodded and looked down.

"But he's never hit you, has he?"

"What?" For a second she truly did not understand the question. Of course Bobby had never hit her. He would never do something like that. He'd been afraid to hold her hand for weeks. He was tender and steady, and he would never lay a hand on her in anger. He'd rather die. He said so himself."No. No. He's not like that."

"No." Audrey's tone held an odd sadness. "Not anymore. That's what he was before he came to know the Lord." She paused and smiled. "His conversion was quite dramatic. Down on his knees in front of the whole church, crying out for God to forgive him. Has he told you about it?"

Tears pricked, and she shook her head.

"Then he started going to AA, and he asked Brent to be his sponsor."

Meagan shook her head. "But why? I mean, why Brent?"

"Brent underwent a similar conversion." Audrey shrugged. "I think Bobby just realized that he needed someone who had been there to help walk him through it."

"And you?" Meagan asked softly. "After how he treated you, you were OK with that?"

A blunt little laugh slipped from Audrey, and she shook her head. "No. I had a hard time with it. But God called me to forgive him. Who was I not to? I hadn't lived a spotless life, either."

"I guess no one has."

Bobby's truck rumbled back to life outside. In a minute he'd leave. He'd go back to his mother's house and she'd be here, separated from him, her family, her son, and everyone she knew until tomorrow.

"So, what do you think of Blithe Settlement so far?" Audrey's perceptive smile underscored her loaded question.

How was she supposed to answer that? She couldn't truthfully say she found the town delightful. But to be honest would only insult its residents. She felt a smile emerge. "I think it's still too soon to tell."

Audrey laughed at that. "I bet it doesn't even begin to compare with a city like Lubbock."

"Well..."

"It's OK, Meagan. No one is more aware of the disadvantages of a small town than I am. And Blithe

Settlement maybe has a few more than most."

"We stopped at the...um...Prickly Pear for dinner." She grinned again at the name. But her grin faded quickly at the memory of the customers there. "No one spoke to him. It seemed like everyone recognized him, but no one stopped to say hello or ask where he's been or what he's been doing. Only the waitress seemed pleased to see him at all. Everyone else just seemed...stunned."

Audrey sighed deeply, seeming to understand. "Bobby made the right decision in leaving here. I think it's hard for people here to accept that he's changed, you know?"

Meagan shook her head. No, she didn't know.

"The Kerr family has been what it is for as long as anyone can remember. Generations." Audrey picked at a spot on the arm of her chair and thought for a moment. "Bobby's grandfather was the town drunk in his day, and his son carried on the tradition. So Bobby and Tommy just followed that path, too."

"The sins of the father..." Meagan whispered the idea and squeezed her eyes shut against the sudden overwhelming fear of what that concept might mean for her own son and his father.

"Exactly." Audrey agreed. "It was just expected of him. But now he's not that man anymore. And I don't think people know how to react." She paused and shook her head. "As much as Brent and I didn't think he should go, leaving here was the right thing for him. It seems like Lubbock really did provide him with the fresh start he needed. I hate to think what might have become of him if he had stayed."

Bobby closed the front door and listened to the heavy sound of his footsteps as he walked through his mother's old house to the kitchen. She was there, just as he knew she would be. For as long as he could remember, she'd spent the majority of her days in the kitchen, either cooking, or cleaning, or sitting at the table. There was no longer a need for her to hide in here, now that her husband presented no threat. But habits died hard, sometimes.

She was just washing the last few dishes and stacking them in the drain rack on the counter when he tossed his keys onto the table. The sound startled her and she jumped and spun around, looking vastly relieved to discover it was him standing in the middle of the room.

He pushed his fingers through his hair and ended the gesture by rubbing the back of his neck. "Sorry. Didn't mean to scare you."

"Oh, that's OK." His mother turned back to the sink, turned the water off, and dried her hands on a dishtowel. "It just seemed for a second like maybe..."

"Like maybe *he* was here?"

She gripped the edge of the counter and sighed, her shoulders sagging.

"I think, under the circumstances, it's OK for you to be relieved he's gone."

Turning around again quickly, she fixed him with a steady, tearful stare. "I'm not relieved. He was my husband for more than forty years. You didn't know him like I did."

"I don't have to know him like you did." Bobby pulled out a chair and sat down. "I know what he made me."

"He made you what his father made him. You, and Tommy, both. And Tommy's doin' a good job of making the same thing out of those boys of his. It never ends."

As she pulled out a chair and sat down adjacent to him, Bobby slowly began to shake his head. "I can't believe that." He said the words more to himself than to her. He had changed. Despite what his father had made him, God had taken a hold and made something better.

"You've done all right for yourself, Bobby." She reached across the table and patted his arm. "I'm proud of you for quitting drinking, and going to church, and getting a good job. You've done all right. And that girlfriend of yours is real pretty, and she seems real sweet. Real upper class. I can understand why you don't want her spending too much time with us."

"It's Tommy I don't want her spending much time with. And it's...it's just this house. It's like he'll always be here, and I don't want him to have any influence on her."

His mother nodded, and Bobby sat quietly, listening to the sounds of cicadas and crickets coming in through the open kitchen window.

"How's your job?"

Bobby shrugged and glanced away. "Good. It's a good job."

"And you have a nice place there in Lubbock?"

"It's just a little one-bedroom apartment. It's nice enough, I guess."

"And Meagan?"

He turned his full attention back to her. It was natural for his mother to have questions about the woman he'd brought home. But talking about Meagan here made him feel like looking over his shoulder, as if there were someone there he wanted to keep the information from.

"You're serious about her?"

Picking up his keys, he shrugged. "I don't know. I guess." He was serious about her. He'd never been more serious. But did he want to share that with his family? Probably not.

"Serious enough to stay in Lubbock for good?"

"I never said I'd come back." He turned the keys over and over, running his finger over the grooves.

"I know," she whispered. "It's just..."

He tore his gaze from the object in his hands and glanced back at his mother. "It's just what?"

She sighed heavily and shook her head, as if to dismiss the subject. Then, when he didn't make an effort to pry the information from her, she continued reluctantly. "It's just that with your father gone...I don't know. There were times he wasn't good to me, but otherwise he took care of me. And now..."

And now you'll be on your own. Bobby wanted to finish the thought for her. She might not phrase it just that way, but that was the point just the same. She wanted to know who would take care of her now.

"Well, you know your brother. I can't depend on him, and he's got his own family to look after. And Hope...well, the last time I saw her she swore she'd never set foot in this house again. I doubt she'll even make it for the funeral tomorrow. And Nicole is just plain wild, always off doing her own thing. No time for anyone but her." She paused and looked down at the table, tracing a seam in the wood with her fingertip.

"But you, Bobby. You're the dependable one. You always have been."

"Mom, I have a job in Lubbock."

"I know, hon, but I could sure use your help around here right now. Just until everything gets settled."

"Mom, I—"

"Maybe you could take some time off."

"It's not that kind of job. I can't just take time off whenever I feel like it."

"Just give it some thought, would you, hon?" Still she wouldn't look at him. "I need you around here. You're the only one I've ever been able to depend on. I can't tell you how hard it's been since you've been gone."

The chair scraped across the floor as he rose to his feet and crossed to the sink. His parents had called him many things in the course of his life, but dependable had never been one of them. He couldn't fathom what she was talking about. Not too many years ago, in fact, he remembered a conversation between the two of them which took place in this very room, and in which she'd called him a freeloader and told him he needed to get his life together before she gave up on him altogether. Now he'd always been the dependable one? Now she needed him?

Bobby took a glass from the drain rack and crossed to the refrigerator. "Is there any tea?"

"In the door."

There it was, right where she'd said it would be when he pulled the door open. But the pitcher of tea wasn't what commanded his attention. It was the half a six pack set prominently on the top shelf, as if it had been put there just for him at just this moment when he wanted nothing more than to reach in and grab one.

He took a deep breath and shut the door, fighting every urge to tear it open again and dive right in with all his heart.

"You change your mind, hon? I can make some coffee if you'd rather."

He shook his head. "No. No, I think I'll just have a glass of water and go on up to bed, if that's all right with you."

His little sister had the right idea. He should never have set foot in this town again.

಄ೕ

The clock on the bedside table said 3:37 a.m.

Bobby pushed off the bed and crossed the room to open the window. He'd forgotten how stuffy it got up here on the second floor when the weather turned hot. The house had central air, but for economic reasons it only got turned on during the hottest weather, and even then it never seemed to make a difference upstairs. At least with the window open he'd get a little breeze. The train whistled off in the distance. It wouldn't be long before it got here, at which point it would have awakened him if he had been able to sleep. He propped one arm up against the wall and stared out at the moonlit yard.

Meagan was probably sleeping soundly at Brent's house. At least he hoped she was. She shouldn't be losing sleep over this, but under any other circumstances he'd pick up the phone and call her. He turned and his gaze drifted to the phone. He couldn't call her now, no matter how desperately he wanted to hear her voice. To hear her say she loved him.

What had possessed him to bring her here, and then leave her at Audrey's? If he did call, she might not talk to him, anyway. Audrey had probably already filled her in completely. That would be for the best. She'd have cold, hard proof that what he'd told her about himself was true. Not that she'd need any after meeting his family, especially Tommy. At least she'd never meet his father.

He ran a hand over his forehead and eyes, then crossed back to the bed, sitting heavily on the edge. His father was gone, and his mother was alone now. Tommy and Nicole were both too disturbed to be any help to her at all, and Hope...he didn't know where she was or if she'd ever be back.

Maybe it was his responsibility to come back here and see that things got settled. Maybe it was his duty to take care of his mother. How would he know? He didn't know the first thing about duty.

He took a deep breath and heaved a heavy sigh, swinging his legs back up onto the bed and leaning back against the pillows. Meagan would take care of her mother. Not that her mother would expect her to. But she'd do it.

But his mother didn't need taking care of. His father had been all but completely useless when it came to finances and taking care of family business. She'd always done that. So why she'd suddenly gone so needy didn't make any sense to him. Maybe she just wanted him to come home, and she couldn't think of any other way to persuade him. Maybe he *should* just come home. He could quit drinking and clean himself up, and get a job, and a place, and a girlfriend in the big city. But deep down inside he'd never amount to anything but this, anyway—this town, this house, this family.

The train whistled again, closer this time, sounding both familiar and foreign. He glanced at the clock again. 3:40 a.m. He shut his eyes tight, willing his mind to dwell on something, anything, other than the alcohol he knew his brother had left for him downstairs in the refrigerator.

∞∞

Meagan started awake, knowing that some sound had disturbed her already fitful sleep, but not knowing exactly what it was. She propped up on her elbows and held her breath, listening. But there was nothing. No sound, except a very distant train whistle.

She rolled onto her side and reached for the watch she'd left on the bedside table, barely managing to stifle a groan. 3:40 a.m. If she didn't get more sleep than this, she wasn't going to be any good at all to Bobby tomorrow.

She flopped onto her back again, clasping hands behind her head. Bobby was probably sleeping comfortably at his mother's house, in his old room. Would he have drifted off thinking of her, or Audrey? Who was she kidding? He wasn't sleeping any better than she. She could almost feel him tossing and turning, glancing at the clock every few minutes, wondering how much longer the night could possibly last. The question of who occupied his thoughts still remained, however.

She closed her eyes, wanting him to be thinking of her. She would will herself into his heart and mind if she thought it possible. But his heart and mind might never be completely open to her, and there was so much about him she didn't know. Standing face to face with his brother, who looked so much like him, had been like meeting his evil twin. Tommy was downright frightening, and she couldn't reconcile them as brothers. Her mind just couldn't make that work.

She sighed heavily and opened her eyes again as the train whistled softly in the distance. One thing was certain; he didn't want her here. He didn't want her to see this part of himself. And now that she was here, she regretted seeing it, because this truly wasn't him anymore.

She reached for her watch again. 3:45. It felt like morning would never come.

11

Bobby reached for her hand as they walked side by side through the unbelievably green cemetery grass. The familiar way he intertwined his fingers with hers gave Meagan a measure of comfort.

"I'm sorry more people didn't come."

He glanced at her, squinting against the early afternoon sunlight, then turning to survey the twenty or so people dispersing from the grave site. "I didn't expect *this* many people."

"Audrey didn't come." Heat rushed to her face, and she didn't dare look at him to watch his response.

His grip on her hand tightened. "Why would she?"

She shrugged. "Why wouldn't she?"

He stopped abruptly, and she turned to face him. Maybe now wasn't the best time to bring this up. But he had to know she would notice Audrey's absence, especially since Brent had come. And even if he had asked Brent to ask Audrey to keep quiet about him, how could he believe she actually would. He had to know that taking her to their home would change everything. He couldn't possibly think that she'd spend the whole night there and the connection between him and Audrey wouldn't come up.

"What did she tell you?"

She searched his face for a long moment, trying to

detect something of his mood in his expression. But it betrayed nothing; no trace of anger, or grief, or any emotion. Then his jaw muscle twitched once, then twice.

"Oh, Bobby." She took his other hand in hers and stepped closer. "She didn't have to tell me anything. I already knew."

"What?" Shock registered on his face, making her feel a little better about his state of mind.

"I knew who she was the second you introduced her to me." She looked down at their joined hands fighting back the tears.

"How?"

"You called me by her name once. When we were at the park, and you ran off to catch Jay." She lifted her gaze to meet his. "You called me Audrey."

His shoulders sagged and he groaned. "Why didn't you say anything?"

"I didn't see the point. I didn't think I'd ever actually meet her."

A long moment passed in which he didn't say anything. His only movement was the expansion of his chest with every deep breath he took.

He withdrew his hands from hers and folded his arms across his chest. "So she didn't give you the details? A blow by blow account? Did she show you her scars?"

"Is that what you wanted her to do? Was that the whole point?" Her voice sounded tight and small. A hot tear slid down her cheek. "It wouldn't have made a difference even if she had."

The way you looked at her is what nearly broke my heart. The thought almost slipped out along with more tears. But she took control with a sniff and a toss of her head. She dabbed at her eyes and nose with the tissue she'd been waiting to use all morning, then she took a deep breath and squared her shoulders.

Bobby's demeanor softened. He reached out and took one of her hands again. "I'm sorry, Meagan. Hard as I try, I just can't ever seem to—"

"Well now! *There's* somethin' I never thought I'd hear a male member of the Kerr family say."

Meagan started as Bobby spun around to face the source of the comment; a small woman with short, shaggy red hair.

"Hope?" Bobby's tone was incredulous. But he broke into a grin anyway. "Is that you? Where've you been? What did you do to your hair?"

"Yes, it's me. I've been in the hill country. And, what's the matter, don't you like it?" She shook her head and ran a hand through her hair. "More importantly, you should introduce me to the woman who rates an apology from a brother of mine."

"This is Meagan. Meagan, this is my sister, Hope."

Meagan extended her hand and Hope took it, pulling her closer.

"You look good." Bobby's sister studied her. "No scars, no bruises. You *are* crying, however, which leads me to wonder..."

Meagan pulled her hand from the other woman's grasp and stepped back to his side, linking her arm through his. "I always cry at funerals."

A slow, appreciative smile made its way across Hope's face, and something in her expression changed.

"Mom will be glad you're here."

Hope shook her head. "Not likely. I'm not staying."

"When are you leaving?"

"Now."

"You should at least come back to the house for dinner."

Hope shook her head even more emphatically. "No way. I didn't come back here to get roped back into this family."

"Then why did you?"

"To make sure it was true. To make sure he was really gone."

Bobby nodded.

Meagan had to stifle a gasp, not only at Hope's statement, but also at Bobby's matter of fact response. What kind of man must their father have been for one child to come to the funeral only to make sure he was really dead, and another to completely understand that reason?

"But you've been back home, haven't you?" Hope narrowed her eyes and cocked her head to one side. "You *have*. And Mom's already started working on you."

Meagan glanced at Bobby, and he looked away as if to survey the landscape. She turned to Hope. "What do you mean?"

"Daddy's problems were apparent." Hope lowered her voice in the patient manner of one explaining something to someone who has no clue. "Everyone could see them. On Mom, on us. But Mom's ways of harming her children...well, they aren't quite so obvious."

She turned back to Bobby and continued. "She's probably already got you thinking that she's lost, with two worthless kids who live here, and one even more worthless who ran off and won't come home. She needs someone to take care of her, right?" She let slip a derisive snort. "Just like Dad always took care of her.

"The smartest thing you ever did was leave here, Bobby. I hear you're not drinkin' anymore. You've got a good steady job. You've got yourself a nice girlfriend, and you're obviously pretty good to her. How long do you think that's gonna last if you come back here? You've changed—"

"Then why does it matter *where* I live? Or where you live? If we really change what does geography have to do with it?"

Meagan couldn't tear her gaze from Bobby's face. She choked back another gasp at the question.

Hope raised her hands in mock surrender. "All I'm saying is, I hear you've got a nice life now. Don't give it up to come back here. I sure don't intend to."

Brother and sister stood, staring at each other for a long moment, at an indefinable impasse. They both had departed here to start fresh elsewhere. So, at some point they would have agreed the best place to be was anywhere but here. But now they seemed at odds on the issue. And it felt like Bobby's mind was the one changing.

On a long sigh his features softened, and he smiled at his sister. "So, you've got a nice life now?"

"It's not perfect. But, compared to what it was this time last year, yeah. Real nice."

"You been going to church?"

"Don't start, Bobby."

He raised one hand in a gesture that promised he'd back off and wrapped the other arm around Meagan's shoulders. She barely felt it. *Why should it matter where I live?* The words still echoed through her mind and heart even though the conversation had moved on.

"You should come back to the house for dinner. It doesn't mean you're moving in. It just means you're coming to dinner." Bobby's voice sounded strained. Which was exactly how she felt.

"Will Tommy be there?"

Bobby's laugh sounded ironic. "I'm sure he will."

Hope took a deep breath and shook her head. "No. I'd just as soon be heading home. I'm glad you're doing so well, and it was nice to meet you Meagan."

She forced a smile.

"You should give me a call sometime," Bobby said as Hope turned and started up a slight slope toward a small pickup truck.

She turned back and grinned. "Sure. But where? Here, or in Lubbock?" With a wave, she turned around again and trotted the rest of the way. Within a moment's time Hope was gone.

Meagan watched her truck wind its way down the cemetery road back to the highway in the distance, until the warm pressure of Bobby's hand at her elbow reminded her of why she'd come with him in the first place. She turned to face him.

"Please tell me you're not thinking of moving back here." It took a great effort to keep her voice steady and calm.

"Everyone else has already gone back to the house." Bobby's grip on her arm tightened as he tried to lead her toward the pickup, but she dug in her heels and gritted her teeth.

"Tell me you're *not* thinking of leaving Lubbock to come back here. Of leaving *me* to come back *here!*"

"I wasn't thinking of leaving you, Meagan." Again, he tried to urge her to his truck. His grip on her elbow tightened a little more, and the pressure with which he pulled her toward him increased.

She pulled her arm out of his grasp. "Well, if you thought maybe I'd move here, you thought wrong."

He turned to face her, the lines of his face setting stonily as he folded his arms across his chest. "And why is that? Because this trashy little town is beneath you? Because my family fits right in here, and you don't want to be part of it? This is where I come from, Meagan. This is who I am. Maybe I belong here."

"This is *not* where you belong!" She reached out to him, laying her hands on his still folded arms, clinging to him as if she could snatch him back from some brink. "You belong in Lubbock with me and Jay."

He turned from her. "We should go. They'll wait to start the meal until we get there."

"You don't belong here, Bobby. This is not who you are anymore."

"That's enough." He turned and pointed sharply at her, taking a deep breath through his nose. "We can talk about this when I take you back home tomorrow."

Her jaw dropped. "And then what?! You'll pack your things and turn around and come right back? When you take me home? What's that supposed to mean?" She stood staring at him, so upset she trembled. "Bobby..." Her voice quavered when she continued despite her effort to sound firm. She didn't even know what she wanted to say, just that she had to convince him. But she'd said too much already.

"I said that's enough!" The temper that he always held so tightly in check exploded as he stalked toward her, anger contorting his features until she hardly recognized him.

She'd never wanted to turn and run away from anything so badly in her whole life. Suddenly he looked just like his brother. She tried to stand her ground but couldn't. She took one step back and then another, which seemed only to anger him further. Her hands went up defensively as she continued to back away.

When he caught up his hands wrapped around her wrists like shackles, his grip so tight she gasped. He gave her a hard shake and her head snapped back, then forward again. But as suddenly as he'd turned on her, he let her go, starting and jumping back as if he'd just received an electric shock.

She stood shaking, watching him for a long moment, afraid to move. His breath came as raggedly and rapidly as hers. Finally, he opened both hands, palms up and stared down at them.

"Don't you see, Meagan?" His voice was hoarse and thick. "As hard as I try...this is what I am. I knew this would happen someday."

She shook her head, tears beginning to overflow. "No. No." She stepped toward him and reached out to touch him again, but he withdrew quickly and turned from her. "This is what everyone here *expects* you to be."

"Because it's what I am." He sounded defeated. "It's what my father was, it's what my brother is, it's what my sister has settled for...and there's no escaping it."

She closed the distance between them and laid both hands on his back. "Yes, there is. It's that highway over there, going west." Sliding her arms around his waist she rested her head against the back of his shoulder. "Let's leave this afternoon, Bobby. Let's go back to your mom's house, say good-bye to everyone, get our things together, and leave today. Right now.

We'll be home before it even gets dark."

He raised one hand to cover hers where she had linked them around his waist and turned his head toward her. "I wanted to hit you just now, Meagan." The despair in his voice brought fresh tears to her eyes. "I could see how scared you were, but I almost couldn't stop myself."

"But you did stop yourself," she said softly, giving him a squeeze for emphasis. "You did. And that's how everyone does it. Do you think I've never wanted to hit anyone? My ex left me with fifteen thousand dollars of debt. If he showed up on my front doorstep tomorrow, don't you know I'd be tempted to slap him across the face? There have been times Jay has tried my patience until I wanted to pick him up and shake him until his teeth rattled."

Bobby's breathing had returned to a normal rhythm, and his thumb traced and retraced a path across her knuckles. He was listening.

"Let's go home, Bobby."

He gave his head a slight shake. "Mom needs me to help her get things settled."

"Let Tommy and Nicole do that."

"They won't. And she won't ask them."

"She would if you weren't here."

He stood silently for a long moment.

Please, Lord. Help him. Make him listen.

Finally he stirred and turned to face her. He searched her eyes and studied her face for minutes, it seemed, before he spoke. "We should get back to the house. We'll talk about this after lunch."

Meagan sighed and nodded. It was something. She'd rather he put his arms around her and promise to leave right away. To get as far from this town, as quickly as possible. But talking about leaving after lunch was the next best thing. At least he was willing to talk about it.

܀ை܀

Lunch time passed uneventfully enough. Meagan kept a wary eye on Tommy, however. Mostly because he seemed to be keeping an eye on her. He kept drinking, too, taking beer after beer from the case in the refrigerator.

Now Tommy stood on the other side of the kitchen fixing a level stare on her, not seeming to care about the conversation going on between his mother and brother, but never truly disengaging from it either. She shifted her weight uncomfortably and tried to press herself closer to Bobby's side. But Tommy's stare was relentless.

The phone rang and Bobby's mother rose and left the kitchen to answer it.

"You about ready to go?" Bobby turned his head toward her to ask the question, but his arms remained folded firmly across his chest.

Meagan nodded. "Mm-hm."

"I think we'll go on and head back home tonight."

Her heart jumped at the words.

"I'll just go and get my things together. Then we'll go on to Brent's and say goodbye."

She nodded. "OK."

He pushed away from the counter against which they were leaning. She watched him go, listened to the sound of his footsteps as he walked through the living room and up the stairs. Relief flooded her heart, and she glanced down to cover the smile she couldn't suppress. He'd decided. He intended to go back home to Lubbock with her. They would leave here, put this place behind them, and everything would be fine.

Thank you, God!

"Those kids sure are quiet." Tommy spoke without taking his eyes from Meagan's face. He leaned one shoulder against the refrigerator and took a long sip from the can in his hand."Laurel, why don't you go on out back and see what they're up to."

"Oh, they're fine." Laurel drawled.

"I said go on." He sounded congenial enough. But she heard a subtle, dangerous note in his tone. He expected to be obeyed. "Go check on them."

Laurel dropped her eyes to the table, then rose to do as he said. Meagan looked back at Tommy, and he grinned at her. She couldn't stay here, alone in this room with him. Bobby was upstairs, and Mrs. Kerr was just a room or two away. He wouldn't dare try anything with other people so close. And even if he did, it would only take a single cry of distress to bring someone to her aid. But panic rose like bile. She had to get out of here.

"I think I'll go upstairs and help Bobby." She crossed the kitchen toward the living room, but Tommy stepped into the doorway, blocking her path.

"He's a grown man. He can pack a little overnight bag by himself."

He didn't touch her. But he also didn't intend to let her pass without harassment; that much was obvious. He raised the can to his mouth and drained it, then he set it on the counter beside him.

"I'd really like to get by—"

"Do I make you nervous, Meagan?"

Tommy's question came out sounding absolutely

sincere. As if he couldn't fathom such a thing. As if he didn't relish doing everything in his power to make her nervous. But how was she supposed to answer? Did she tip her hand and tell the truth? Or should she lie and say no?

"Tell me how you and my brother met. No, wait! Let me guess." He grinned. "At church. Right?"

She swallowed and shook her head. "I cut his hair."

"Oh." Tommy drew the syllable out as if some great mystery had just been solved. "Oh. So you cut hair for a living."

"That's right."

"And that's how you two met. He came to you for a haircut."

That's what I just said, isn't it? She bit back the sarcastic question and looked down. The last thing she wanted to do was provoke him.

"That's a mighty common job for such a pretty, upper class woman like you." Her hair tickled her collarbone as he reached out and picked up a lock of it, smoothing it, caressing it with his fingers. "But I guess I should have known, pretty as your hair is." She took a quick step back and fought against the urge to slap his hand away. The smell of the beer on his breath made her stomach turn.

"Tell me something, Miss Meagan." He laid a hand gently on her shoulder and slid it down her arm in a sleazy caress as her skin crawled. "You think a woman like you could ever be interested in a man like me?"

Meagan shuddered inwardly. "No."

His eyebrows shot up and he grinned. "No, huh? And why is that?" His hand traveled up her arm and back down again.

"Because you're married." That was probably *last* on her list of reasons. But, hopefully, he would find it the least provoking.

Sure enough, he threw his head back and laughed. "Come on." Before she had time to outmaneuver him, he'd grabbed her arm and was ushering her toward the back door. "Let's go on outside and find a nice quiet place to sit and talk awhile."

Meagan tried to stand her ground but his grip on her arm was firm and the more she resisted the tighter it became.

"Come on." His pleasant tone of voice contradicted the rough way he pulled her across the room.

"No!" She wrenched her arm free and stepped toward the door, out of his reach. "Thank you. But I think I'll just go and see if Bobby needs any help."

Meagan spun around, ready to flee, and ran right into Bobby. *Thank you, Lord!* She followed her first impulse and clutched the front of his shirt, clinging to him, as his arms closed around her.

"Everything all right?" He glanced from her to Tommy and back again. "What's going on? Where's Laurel?"

"She went out back to check on the kids," Tommy drawled casually. "Me and Meagan were just fixing to sit down and talk a little bit."

She straightened and pushed herself out of Bobby's embrace. She had panicked and clung to him like a scared little girl. How could she recover so the situation didn't escalate further? She rubbed her arm just above the elbow where Tommy had grabbed her, still feeling the pressure of his fingertips digging into the flesh.

She glanced at Bobby to find him studying the red skin where Tommy's fingers had clutched her arm. Meagan dropped both her hands and clasped them in front of her. All she wanted to do was leave. As long as there wasn't any trouble between Bobby and Tommy, the two of them could be out of here and on their way home.

"Meagan?" Bobby's solid voice drew her gaze to his face. "Is everything OK?"

"I'm all right. Let's just go." She looked away. He'd be able to see the remains of panic in her eyes if she looked at him. He'd know something happened, and that would just prolong their time here. Who was she kidding? He already knew something happened. She could tell by the stiffness of his posture, the ragged rhythm of his breathing.

A glance at Tommy confirmed that suspicion. He'd taken a seat at the table and leaned brashly back, shooting a glare at Bobby that dared him to do something about it.

"Bobby, hon, are you leaving already?"

Meagan started and glanced at his mother, whose stricken glance vacillated between Bobby and the bag he'd set down on the floor beside him.

"Um, yeah. We're gonna head on back."

"But, Bobby—"

"I'll call you when I get home."

Karen nodded, but her disappointment was apparent. She shot an accusatory, disapproving glance at Meagan, but covered it quickly with a smile. "I'm so glad we all got to meet you, Meagan." She crossed the kitchen and gave her a stiff hug. "I hope we get to see you again real soon."

"Thank you." Meagan's voice was soft, and she could barely make eye contact with anyone. "It was good to meet you, too."

"Y'all drive safe." Karen hugged Bobby next. "And be sure and let me know when you'll be back home, baby. I could sure use your help around here."

"I'll call you later." Bobby's voice sounded terse. He turned without another word to his brother, leading Meagan toward the front door with a firm hand planted in the small of her back.

It felt as if a weight lifted from her as she climbed up into his pickup. They were going home. Everything would be all right.

12

There was so much he needed to discuss with her. Not the least of which was what had gone on between her and Tommy during the five minutes he'd been out of the room. Bobby took a deep breath and shifted in his seat, turning to glance out the driver's side window. Plenty of times in his life, he wanted to beat his brother to a senseless pulp. Plenty of times he'd tried, too. But the desire to drag him outside and pound him into oblivion had never been quite as appealing as when Meagan had come flying out of the kitchen and into his arms just a few hours ago.

Bobby glanced at her. She'd leaned back and dozed off about thirty minutes ago, and the urge to reach over and trace the line of her cheekbone was almost irresistible. But he didn't want to wake her. Her face was the picture of peace and trust, and he couldn't bring himself to spoil it. Not again. An image imposed itself, of her beautiful eyes open wide in fear and panic—opening to see him as he truly was for the first time. It was an expression he'd seen hundreds of times, on his mother's face, his sisters', Audrey's, numerous other girlfriends' faces. But never on Meagan's. Until today, when he'd seen it on her twice. First when he'd clamped his fingers around the soft flesh of her arms at the cemetery. Bobby gripped the steering wheel tighter, as if he could squeeze the image out of existence. He didn't have a clue what had snapped inside him. But something had, and he almost struck her. *Why, God?*

Meagan had only wanted him to go home with her. She had only been trying to convince him that he was no longer the very thing he'd turned out to be. She loved him, and she'd been trying to build him up. And he'd repaid her faith with violence. The panic stricken look on her face stopped him. That look had reflected so clearly what he was deep down inside, underneath all the talk of faith and the new, clean lifestyle.

That same panicked look had greeted him when he'd come downstairs. Bobby glanced over at Meagan as she stirred and sighed. She'd been in a hurry to get out of that room, and she'd been alone there with Tommy, so there was no way to tell what happened. The look on her face had been all the proof he needed, not only that Tommy had done or said something to frighten her, but also that he himself hadn't really changed at all.

Bobby expelled a weary breath. So why hadn't he snapped then, and unleashed his fury on someone who deserved it? How could he maintain such control when the woman he loved had been threatened in some way, but not when she herself was expressing a totally valid argument? Meagan shifted again beside him, and he glanced over to find her studying him with sleepy eyes.

"What are you thinking about?" she murmured.

He shrugged and shook his head. "Nothing much."

"Tommy?"

He clenched his jaw and nodded. "Among other things."

"He didn't hurt me, Bobby." She raised her head from the seat.

"No?" He glanced pointedly to the bruise on her arm where his brother had obviously had his hands on her.

Meagan followed his glance and shrugged as she rubbed the spot. "Jay has given me worse bruises than that."

"Don't make excuses!" The vehemence in his voice startled him. One glance at Meagan told him it startled her, too. He sighed. "I'm sorry. I didn't mean to yell. I just...it's just the thought that he put his hands on you...and that I did it earlier, too... Meagan, I'm sorry for what I did at the cemetery. Please believe me..."

"Oh, Bobby." The tenderness in her voice brought an ache to his throat. "Have you been sitting there thinking about that the whole way home?"

He swallowed and stared out the windshield for a long moment before giving her a brief nod.

He couldn't suppress a burdened sigh when he felt the warmth of her hand on his arm. "We all do things that aren't like us sometimes. Especially when we're stressed."

It was all he could do to keep from hanging his head and letting his shoulders sag. She just didn't get it. What he'd done today had been *just* like him. Just like the *real* him.

For all he tried to convince himself that he was a different man now, no force on this earth could change where he came from, or who his father was.

I'm your Father now.

Bobby stretched and rotated his shoulders, working out the stiffness of a four hour drive. Yes, he'd heard all the encouraging, religious answers from people like Brent who had been there before. And he knew what the Bible said about salvation.

"Therefore, if anyone is in Christ, he is a new creation; the old has gone, the new has come!"

It was one of the first verses he'd learned. He'd clung to it those first few months, when he realized that good intentions and AA meetings weren't enough; that on his own, he wasn't a strong enough man to pull himself up out of the hell that had been his life. But he'd never truly change. How could he after so many years? How was it possible when the habits of the old man still pulled so powerfully?

"Bobby." Meagan reached for his hand.

Ordinarily, the soft sound of her voice when she said his name, and the smoothness of her skin when she held his hand either warmed and comforted him, or lit a fire he found increasingly more difficult to resist, a desire he wouldn't have hesitated to act upon not too long ago. Now it just underscored his heartache. No part of him deserved her. And no part of her deserved all the ways in which he knew he'd end up hurting her. And then there was Jay…what kind of father could he possibly be to Jay? He'd probably end up ruining him. No. He'd rather die. And leaving them would probably kill him. But their future would be brighter and safer if he weren't a part of it. He glanced sideways at her and tried to smile through his breaking heart.

"I love you," she said softly.

"Oh, Meagan." The words slipped out before he could stop them, and he heard the hoarse anguish in his own voice. "I love you, too."

Meagan didn't have the slightest idea what was going on inside Bobby's head. But she did have the distinct impression that it wasn't good. She stole a glance at him as she unlocked her front door. But the stony lines of his face gave nothing away.

She pushed the door open and stepped across the threshold. Dusky light filtered in through the closed blinds, and though the house wasn't yet dark, Meagan stopped to switch on a lamp. She started at the sound of the front door closing behind her, and she turned sharply just to make sure he hadn't left.

He glanced at her as he set her small suitcase down by the hall door. "Thanks for going with me, Meagan."

That's it? He'd barely spoken to her on their drive home. And when she thought she'd finally convinced him to talk about what was on his mind, he clammed up again. And now he stood awkwardly, looking like he wanted to leave, thanking her cordially for going with him. Like she was nothing more than an acquaintance who had done him a favor.

She tossed her keys into her purse, and then the purse to a chair. "Bobby..." She spun to face him, not even knowing what she wanted to say.

Now he stood, hands on hips, looking at her expectantly. She gritted her teeth. "I just wish you'd talk to me!"

He looked down.

"You hardly said anything the whole way home." Unexpected tears sprang to her eyes. "It felt so awkward. It's like suddenly we don't know each other. I know something's bothering you. And I know that it's more than what happened at the cemetery. I just...I just wish you'd tell me what it is. Have I done something wrong?"

He glanced back up at her and took a deep breath, like he wanted to say something. But still he remained silent, flexing his hands then balling them into fists at his sides.

"Is it Tommy? I'll tell you everything he said to me, Bobby. I just didn't want to make an issue of it there because I didn't want there to be any trouble. I just wanted us to leave."

The muscle at his jaw began to tense and relax. His eyes narrowed.

Say something! She wanted to scream the words at him. She wanted to fling herself into his arms and cling to him, to quell this desperate feeling that something between them was about to go horribly wrong. Instead, she took a deep breath, and then another. It didn't soothe her much, but it did give her a moment to think better of the screaming idea. She sniffed and folded her arms.

"After you went upstairs, Tommy told Laurel to go out back and check on the kids. I told him that I wanted to go upstairs and see if you needed help." She paused and looked down. "But he blocked the door so I couldn't get by. He asked if he made me nervous." Another deep breath did little to stop the chilling effect the memory had on her. "Then he asked how you and I met, and I told him." An involuntary shudder shook her as she remembered how Tommy had touched her.

It was like Bobby looked right into her eyes and read her mind. "Did he touch you?"

She pressed her cool palms to her suddenly blazing cheeks. "Yes." She whispered hoarsely. "When I told him I cut hair, and that's how we met, he touched my hair." She raised a hand and caught a lock of her hair with her fingers.

He took a deep, unsteady breath and tilted his head. "Then what?"

"He asked if I could ever be interested in a man like him." She paused and bit her lower lip. Maybe she should just omit the detail about how Tommy had caressed her arm. She ran a hand up and down the arm, feeling the tender spot just above her elbow where his fingers had left their mark. Bobby already knew. She told him.

"He, um, touched my arm." Tears welled again. "He kind of rubbed his hand up and down. And I told him that I wouldn't be interested in a man like him. He asked why. And I said because he was married."

Bobby's expression changed. Now he looked a little like he was fighting a grin. "You told him you wouldn't be interested in him because he was *married*?"

Meagan nodded quickly. "Well, it's not the only reason. But I figured it would be the one that angered him least."

Bobby did grin then. The tension in her shoulders began to relax and she smiled hesitantly, stepping closer to him. "So you see, nothing really happened."

"How'd you get the bruise?"

She swallowed. "He...um...took me by the elbow. Like this." She reached for Bobby's elbow to demonstrate. "And...um...he said we should go outside and find a quiet place to sit and talk."

Bobby's jaw actually dropped. "You mean he tried to take you from the house."

"Well, he said 'let's go outside and—'"

"You have a bruise, Meagan. You don't get a bruise from a gentle 'let's go outside, shall we?' touch."

He took gentle hold of her elbow to demonstrate what he was talking about. Then his grip tightened and he began to push her across the room. "*This* is how you get a bruise like that. Trust me. I know."

He stopped pushing her, but he didn't release his hold on her arm. "Did he intend to take you out of the house?"

Meagan nodded and looked down. "I think so."

"Oh, Meagan!" He let her go and turned from her, shoving a hand roughly through his hair.

"But he didn't! I jerked myself free and turned to run upstairs, and there you were." She laid both her hands on his back. "Bobby, I would never have gone with him. That's not what you think, is it? Because I would never have—"

With a heavy sigh he turned back and took her into his arms. "I know, baby. I know. It's not your fault. It's mine. I should have never taken you there."

"But nothing happened." She clutched the front of his shirt. "And nothing would have. What could he have done with you and your mother inside the house and Laurel out back?"

Bobby's mouth set into a grim line before he took a breath as if to speak. But he didn't say anything. He just let the breath out and shook his head.

"I'm *glad* I went with you." Her voice broke, and a tear fell. She swiped quickly at it with one hand and then returned her hand to his shirt front. "You might not have come back otherwise. And I just don't know what I'd do if you left, Bobby. I love you so much."

She felt the rough warmth of his hands close around hers, and he searched her face intensely, his expression gradually softening. His gaze came to rest on her mouth for a few excruciatingly long seconds before he covered it with his own.

She nearly melted as she pressed to him, sliding her hands up his chest, around his neck, and into his hair. He slid hands down her back and around her waist, setting her skin on fire through the thin fabric of her dress. It only took a few seconds in his arms to make her heart pound wildly. Her body went numb all the way to her toes only to be brought deliciously back to feeling with every caress of his hands, every touch of his mouth.

He loved her. She could tell by the way he kissed her, the way he touched her, exploring every curve, the way he tried to pull her closer. Her head swam, and the feel of his breath on her skin sent a marvelous series of shivers through her as he started a trail of soft, warm kisses along the length of her throat. *Which direction is up?* She couldn't even tell anymore. His fingertips brushed lightly against her skin as he pushed her hair back over her shoulder. Meagan closed her eyes and arched her neck in anticipation of his continued tender assault on her senses. First one warm, moist kiss, then another, then one in the little hollow where her neck met her collar bone.

Stop.

She opened her eyes. Was that a voice she heard? Had Bobby said it?

No. His mouth covered hers again hungrily. He clearly had no intention of stopping now. Nor did she want him to. She closed her eyes again and gave herself over to him. Something had hurt him in the past two days. Something about his trip home had damaged his heart and shaken his confidence. And if this was the kind of comfort he needed, she was willing to give it gladly. They loved each other. How could it possibly hurt? And if it could stop whatever she sensed was about to go wrong between them, it would be more than worth it.

She reached for his hand and he straightened and met her gaze. His short hair was ruffled adorably, and his eyes bright with need.

"Come on," she said softly, taking him by the hand. Silently she led him through the living room and kitchen to her bedroom. But he stopped in the doorway. She turned around to find him clutching the door facing like it was the only thing keeping him from falling straight into the Devil's Sinkhole.

"Meagan, no. We shouldn't..."

Meagan went back to him, grasped his hands again and pulled him in. "Just kiss me."

There was no hesitancy, no second thought about the way he kissed her, and she returned his passion shamelessly. It had been so long since she'd been kissed this way, touched this way, loved this way. The softness of his mouth on hers, and the stubble of his jaw on her tender skin was almost more than she could take. Tears stung her eyes, and she wanted to cry out loud.

"Stay with me tonight, Bobby," she whispered in his ear. "Mom has Jay, and she's not expecting us home until tomorrow, anyway. Just for tonight."

Her invitation must have stoked the fire within him. He groaned and pulled her hard against him, the heat of his kisses increasing. The next thing she realized was the bed behind her, and that she was sinking gently into it, helping him undo the buttons on the front of her dress between kisses.

Stop!

The single word pierced the thick veil of desire

that had cloaked the rational, practical part of her brain and echoed until it was all she could hear.

Bobby stopped abruptly and pushed up, as if he'd heard it, too. Hovering over her, bracing himself with his arms, he searched her face, almost as if to determine whether she'd been the one who said it.

"Bobby?" She reached up to touch his face with one hand and clutched the front of his shirt with the other. His body was still so close she could feel his warmth. The urge to arch her body toward his almost overwhelmed her, and she knew that's all it would take to bring him back to her.

He pushed off and sat up on the edge of her bed. His gaze traveled over every inch of her body before settling on her face. "We shouldn't do this." He reached for her dress and pulled it closed, tenderly fastening every button with his trembling hands. Then one of his hands slid down to her waist. "I can't do this." He leaned forward then, elbows on his knees and buried his face in his hands.

Meagan sat up beside him and wrapped her arms around his shoulders, on the verge of telling him how much she loved him. But she'd said that already, so many times, and it didn't seem to comfort him right now.

"I should go." He raised a hand to cover hers.

"No, Bobby." She whispered past the ache in her throat. "Stay."

But he only shook his head. "I need to go."

He was up and out of the room almost before she realized it. In the living room he paced agitatedly, pushing aside a stack of magazines on an end table, picking up couch pillows and dropping them haphazardly back into place. "What'd I do with my keys?"

Before she could speak he found them and headed for the door.

"Wait!" She followed close behind him, tears beginning to fall freely down the scorching skin of her cheeks. She wrapped arms around herself to keep from flinging herself at him. This was the exact feeling she had when Kevin left her; this same desperate, hopeless certainty that if he walked out her door now, she would never see him again. "Please don't go."

"I'll call you." Bobby reached for the doorknob, but Meagan couldn't stifle a heart rending sob. He stopped, turned back and met her gaze, then he laid a gentle hand against her cheek, brushing tears away with his thumb. "I'll call you."

"When?" She sniffed and leaned into his touch.

"Soon."

He turned and left without another word.

What had she done wrong? Meagan pressed both hands and forehead to the door after he'd closed it quietly behind him. He was right they shouldn't have let things go that far. But this wasn't something they hadn't talked about before. It wasn't something they couldn't deal with. She balled her hands into fists and let another sob erupt. He was turning away from her, and there was nothing she could do to stop him.

She heard his truck start up and drive away. With it went a piece of her heart.

⤞⤝

God, what have I done?

Bobby shifted the truck into park in his usual spot at his apartment complex. He gripped the steering wheel with both hands then leaned forward, resting his head there.

What have I done?

He'd driven several miles across town and still he couldn't catch his breath, he couldn't relax the tension. He pushed off the steering wheel with a heavy sigh, and leaned back against the driver's seat. Meagan had been so sweet, and soft, and willing. He could still feel her in his arms. The scent of her perfume still lingered on his skin and clothes. His hands still burned from touching her. He raised them and rubbed his face. But closing his eyes was a mistake. The image remained, etched into his mind. Meagan laying there on her bed with her dress half undone and the thin fabric hugging every curve of her long body; it was all he could see. And it did nothing to lessen his impulse to turn this old truck around, go back to her house, and finish what he'd started.

But he couldn't do that to her. He couldn't treat her that way. He was already breaking her heart. He couldn't use her like that knowing he wasn't going to stay with her. The only reason she'd been willing to give herself to him so completely was because she fully expected him to marry her soon. If his father hadn't died...If he hadn't taken her home to meet his hateful family, he would have.

He swallowed down the ache rising in the back of his throat. But what right did he have to complicate Meagan's life by dragging her into his family?

He closed his eyes again and leaned his head back against the headrest. The things his brother might have done to her if he'd gotten her out of the house...*Lord, thank you for keeping her safe.*

Meagan didn't understand men like them. Why should she? She'd never been around any. *"What could he have done...?"* she'd asked. Bobby hung his head and pinched the bridge of his nose to try and stem the flow of images of what Tommy could have done if he'd gotten her off alone someplace.

Tommy had never been outright accused of raping anyone. But chances were good that he had. Bobby squeezed his eyes tight against the tears that threatened. The Lord knew that he had pushed those limits himself once or twice in his past. That Meagan was sweet and innocent of men like them was enough to make Tommy want to spoil it. And that she belonged to someone he hated would just give him that much more motivation.

No! Bobby jerked the keys from the ignition, and got out of the pickup, his decision made. He might not be able to change where he came from or who his people were. But he could make perfectly sure that Meagan was never subjected to them, or Tommy's–or his own, for that matter–unpredictable, violent personality. Ever again.

≈∽≪

Meagan wiped the steam from the bathroom mirror and stared at the red swollen eyes of the woman she saw there. Shame stung every nerve. Bobby hadn't run off because she'd been so willing to make love with him. But she *had* been willing. More than willing. She glanced down at her bare left ring finger. What did that say about her?

She towel dried her hair and ran a comb through it, closing her eyes against the image of Tommy toying with it earlier, and then Bobby brushing it away from her shoulder. She gave a small head shake, trying to clear it. Then she tightened the bathrobe sash, switched off the light, and headed for the kitchen.

She couldn't stop from peeking out the front window. Just to make sure his truck wasn't there. It was a stupid thing to do. And her heart dropped when she discovered the inevitable. He hadn't come back.

But in the kitchen was her answering machine. And on her answering machine was one message. Her heart leapt, and she almost laughed out loud. He had called. He said he would call soon, and he'd called as soon as he got home. She pushed the play button.

"Meagan?" The familiar voice recorded there made her heart break. "It's me. Kevin. I was just calling to let you know that I'm gonna be in Lubbock in a couple of weeks. I was hoping we could get together. Nothing major. You know, just to catch up. I'd like to see Jay. Anyway, I'll call back tomorrow."

How convenient!

Kevin had never wanted to see Jay. Not even right after he'd been born. Her parents and sister had always been there when she needed help. But for the most part, she'd raised Jay by herself. At least until she met Bobby. Bobby and Jay had taken to each other, and she had begun to think of them as a family. Wasn't *that* stupid of her. And now it was falling apart, and suddenly Kevin wanted to see Jay.

Why now?

She snatched up the receiver and dialed her mother's number, fighting to control the desperate ache inside as she listened to the ring at the other end of the line.

"Hello?"

Meagan almost burst into tears at the safe, familiar sound of her mom's voice. She cleared her throat. "Hi,

Mom."

"Hi, honey. How's everything going? How's Bobby?"

Meagan pressed a hand to her mouth as she felt her face contort with emotion. "Bobby's fine. Um, we came home early."

"Honey, what happened?"

"Do you think you could go ahead and keep Jay tonight like we planned, and I'll just come over in the morning? All my appointments are cancelled for tomorrow anyway, so I thought I'd just take the day off."

"Of course. But, Meagan, what's wrong? You sound like you've been crying." There was a long silence. "Is everything OK with Bobby?"

"Oh, Mom." Her voice finally broke and the tears overflowed. "I don't know."

"Honey, do we need to come over? We can be there in fifteen minutes."

"No, Mom. No. I'm OK."

"Caroline got home yesterday. Why don't I send her over? She can spend the night there with you."

"No, really. I...I kind of want to be alone. OK?"

There was a long pause.

"OK." Her mother sounded reluctant. "But you call if you need anything."

"I will. Bye."

She set the phone aside and wiped at the tears. She *didn't* want to be alone. She wanted Bobby here with her, and not necessarily in the capacity she'd originally proposed to him. She wanted him to hold her, and talk to her, and assure her that she was completely wrong in her sudden intuition that, for some inexplicable reason, it was over between them.

13

"...and on top of everything else, guess who called and left a message on my machine last night." Meagan unbuckled Jay from his car seat and stood back to let him scramble out of the car.

"Don't tell me. Kevin." Caroline pulled a few bags of groceries from the back seat. "What's our big spender been up to lately?"

Meagan followed Jay across the carport, pulled open the screen and unlocked the side door, pushing it open for Jay to run inside. "Evidently, he's going to be in Lubbock in a couple of weeks and he wants to get together. He wants to see Jay."

"When it rains, it pours."

She held the screen door open for Caroline, then went back to the car for the last few bags of groceries.

"I should be glad, right?" She slammed the car door a little harder than necessary and hauled the sacks into the kitchen. She glanced around the room to make sure Jay wasn't there, then lowered her voice. "I mean, he's Jay's father. He has a right to at least see him. It'd be better for Jay if they had some kind of relationship. Right?"

"That's what the experts say."

Meagan sighed. Her shoulders sagged and tears threatened. She sniffed and pulled a gallon of milk from a sack, transferring it to the refrigerator. "I just don't know what to do. Here I'd painted all these pictures in my head about how things would be with Bobby, and now...now Kevin wants to see Jay."

A little pair of arms wrapped around her legs, and she reached down to tousle Jay's hair.

"Is Bobby coming over, Mama?"

Meagan drew in a deep breath against the tears which suddenly pooled. "No, I don't think so, baby. Not today." She stroked his hair, pulling his bangs to one side. "You need a haircut." She forced a smile, hoping it would make her sound happier. "How about after your nap, we go out back and I'll give you a haircut."

"No. I don't want a haircut." Jay whined and let go of her legs, sulking out of the kitchen.

"Let's see how you feel after your nap."

She glanced at the answering machine. Two messages. She punched the play button only to be greeted by the voice of one of her debt collector regulars. She pressed delete, and the second message started. But there was only silence, then the click of someone hanging up. She glanced at Caroline.

"Call him." Caroline finished unpacking the last of the groceries and wadded up the plastic bags. "I'll go read Jay a couple of stories and put him down for his nap. You call Bobby."

She left the room, leaving Meagan leaning wearily against the counter, staring at the phone. Why shouldn't she call him? Had Bobby actually said that he thought they should break up? No. So it was totally possible that everything was just fine as far as their relationship was concerned and she had overreacted to his dismal exit last night. Maybe he just needed a little time and space after such a rough trip home.

She snatched up the phone and dialed his work number. But her confidence waned more with each passing ring. She was just about to hang up when someone answered.

"West Texas Feed, this is Todd."

"Um, hi Todd. It's Meagan."

"Oh, hi Meagan. How's it going?"

"OK." She swallowed and cleared her throat. "I was trying to get hold of Bobby."

"He's not here."

She glanced at her watch. "Did he go to lunch?"

"No. He came in this morning and worked till noon or so, then he left. He said he was taking a week of vacation. Something about helping his mother get things settled back home."

What! She wanted to shout. *You mean he went back there!* It felt like someone had just knocked the wind right out of her. Bobby had done just exactly what she tried to convince him not to do. He'd brought her home, dropped her off, and turned right around to go back.

"Oh." She cringed at the shocked tone of her own voice. "Thanks, Todd. Bye."

"Bye."

She hung up, confusion numbing every nerve. What did this mean? If he'd taken a week's vacation, he must intend to come back. But why wouldn't he tell her where he was going? She might not like the decision, but that was no reason to not tell her about it. Unless it really was over between them. She glanced down at the phone in her hand. She could call his cell...

"So, what's the story?"

She started at the sound of her sister's voice.

"He's not at work." Meagan pushed hair behind her ears and sighed. "He took a week of vacation and went back to Blithe Settlement."

"Without telling you?" Caroline pulled a chair out and sat down. "OK. So what does that mean?"

Meagan shrugged and shook her head, crossing to sit adjacent to Caroline. "I don't know. Maybe this is his way of breaking up with me. Just leave and quit calling."

But the pieces were beginning to fall together. His silence on the ride home yesterday? He didn't want to talk to her because there was no point. There was no reason for him to open up to her if he didn't plan on staying with her. Then there was the distant way he thanked her for going with him when they made it home. She squeezed her eyes shut to stop the flow of tears. Maybe that's when he'd intended to say it; that he wanted to break up. If she'd just kept her mouth shut he probably would have.

Then later. *God, forgive me!* In her bedroom when they'd stopped in the nick of time. *We shouldn't do this,* he'd said. *I can't do this.* He'd known then. He'd already planned to break up with her, and he couldn't go through with using her knowing that he wouldn't ever see her again. *Thank you, Lord, for that.*

"Oh, Caroline." She folded arms on the table and laid her head down on top of them. "It's over. That's all there is to it. I should have known better than to get involved with someone."

She willed herself to be angry with him. She shut her eyes tight and tried hard to tap something furious inside, to make his outright rejection not hurt quite so much. But she gave up trying when she felt Caroline's hand stroke her hair gently. All she wanted to do was weep.

"Maybe..." Caroline's soft venture prompted Meagan to look up again. "I mean, with all you told me about his family. Maybe it's for the best. Think about it. If you were to marry him, you'd be part of that family. *Jay* would be part of that family. Maybe—if it *is* over—this is a blessing in disguise."

She looked up and wiped the tears away with her fingers. Caroline was right. There was no way on earth she'd let Jay within five miles of Tommy Kerr or his kids. No way. But Jay had grown attached to Bobby. Twice today he'd asked when he could see him.

They'd just have to quit, cold turkey. No Bobby. No mention of Bobby. If Jay asked again, she'd just have to make herself smile and say he wasn't coming back, but didn't we have fun while he was here?

A fresh batch of tears sprang forth. How was she going to pull *that* off?

"I love him." Meagan whispered, glancing up at Caroline to find her sister's eyes brimming as well. "I thought he was the one."

�๏ఐ

Bobby heard the car doors slamming, and the hollering kids outside about two seconds before the commotion came thundering through the front door and the rest of the house. Tommy had two boys, and neither one had any manners. Bobby watched as they went straight for the Twinkies in the pantry, and the Cokes in the refrigerator, and then headed out the back door, without so much as a "hello" to their grandma.

"You boys stay away from the tracks!" His mother followed them onto the back porch.

Just like his sons, Tommy's first stop was the refrigerator, from which he pulled a can of beer. He popped the top and took a sip, analyzing Bobby over the rim of the can.

"When did you get back in town?"

Bobby didn't move. Didn't answer. He sat right where he was, leaning forward with his arms folded on the table, mentally wrestling with images of Tommy's fingers toying with Meagan's hair, his hand clamping around her arm tightly enough to leave a bruise, his intention to take her from this house and do who knows what to her.

"Day before yesterday," he said finally.

"Where's your girlfriend?"

"Bobby came back to help me get things settled here." His mom stepped between them, setting a glass of iced tea on the table in front of Bobby.

"We met with the insurance agent yesterday, and got all that in order. He called someone to see about coming out and hauling off those old truck carcasses of your Daddy's—"

"Don't get rid of those, Mama!"

"Take them to your place if you want them." Bobby leaned back in his chair and took a long drink of his tea. "She wants to get the place cleaned up a little."

"Look at you." Tommy shot him something between a grin and a sneer. "Drinkin' your iced tea. Why don't you just stick your little pinky out like a girl?"

Ordinarily Bobby would have grinned at the taunt, maybe even laughed. But right now all he wanted to do was get up and put his fist into something.

Tommy's malicious grin widened. He turned and pulled the refrigerator open again.

"Where's Laurel today?" It was his mom's attempt to diffuse the tension. When they'd been kids a change of subject would sometimes work. But the older they got, the less attention they paid to her.

"Aw, she's not feelin' too good this afternoon."

And there it was. The family code. Bobby took a breath and looked down into his tea. If a woman in their family was "not feeling too good," that meant that her man had most likely tied one on the night before and she got in the way. There was no doubt in his mind that Laurel wasn't feeling well. Or that her malaise was the direct result of Tommy's handiwork.

His mom clucked her tongue. "I'll make her up a plate of something and you can take it home to her."

And *that* was her personal part of the code, meaning; "It's the least I can do for raising such a good-for-nothing son."

Tommy turned from the refrigerator and pointedly set a can of beer down on the table in front of Bobby. He even pulled back the tab and opened it.

Lord, help me!

As if he had no control over it, his gaze fastened itself on the open can.

"Oh, go on." Tommy pulled out a chair and sat down. "One little old beer ain't gonna hurt."

"Probably not." He pushed it away. "But I still don't want it."

Tommy's smile looked sinister. *Oh, but you do.* His expression seemed to say.

He did. Bobby swallowed hard. He could almost taste it, could almost feel it sliding down his throat into his body, into his blood, numbing his heart just a little.

"You never did tell me where Meagan is."

Just the sound of her name coming from Tommy's

filthy mouth made him want to come up out of his chair and punch him. He curled his fingers around his tea glass.

"We had ourselves a nice chat before y'all left." Tommy took a long drink from the can in his hand. "She's a real special girl, isn't she? Real pretty. Tall and trim. Long legs. That hair. And all that smooth, soft skin." He drew in a long, deliberate breath and let it out slowly. "Don't know what you did to rate a woman like that."

His heart pounded harder with each of Meagan's physical attributes that Tommy rattled off. He looked down where he clasped his hands to keep them from shaking furiously.

"Yeah." Tommy continued. "I wouldn't mind spending a little more *time* with a woman like that."

Bobby shoved himself out of his chair, toppling it behind him.

"Bobby, honey, Tommy's just trying to get a rise out of you." It was all he could do to fight the impulse to shrug his shoulder out from underneath the hand his mother had laid there. "He doesn't mean it."

"Go on and have a couple." Tommy pointed a lazy finger toward the open beer on the table. "Then we can go out back and settle this like we used to."

"Settle what?!" Bobby withdrew from his mother's touch and braced both arms on the table. "What is it that needs to be settled, Tommy? That I've quit drinking and you haven't? That I've got a steady job and you're a lazy bum? That I've gotten out of this crappy town, and moved on, and found a beautiful woman who's not terrified of me? That I've turned to God? Is that why you hate me so much more all of a sudden? Is it that Dad's gone? Or that you turned out just like him?" He turned his back on his brother and shoved a hand roughly through his hair. Then he turned back to face him again. "Seems to me that's all been settled already."

The only signs that Bobby had hit a nerve at all were the little twitch that had begun at Tommy's jaw, and the subtle fire ignited in his ordinarily bloodshot eyes.

"Did she tell you about our talk?" Tommy went on as if he hadn't heard a word his brother just said. "I tell you, I'd sure like the opportunity to finish it."

An image flashed of Bobby shoving the table out of his way and hauling his brother out of his chair by his shirt front, slamming him into the wall behind him. He tried to blink it away. As if through a will of their own, Bobby's hands had balled into fists at his sides.

"Well you won't get that opportunity," he said finally, through gritted teeth. "Because I don't intend to bring her back here. Ever."

"Aw, don't tell me she didn't like it here." Mock surprise underscored Tommy's words. "We didn't scare her off, did we? She didn't break up with you, did she?"

"Did she, Bobby?" His mother's voice startled him. Usually by this point in a confrontation between him and Tommy, she'd have left the room.

He turned his head in her direction. "She won't be back."

Tommy smiled again as if some evil plan had come to full fruition. "She was too good for you, anyway."

You don't have to tell me *that.*

He almost flinched at the touch of his mother's hand on his back. "It's probably for the best, hon. I mean, I could see right away that she'd never fit in around here. All she'd have done is drag you further and further from us, trying to change you into something you're not. I know she was pretty, and I bet she's real sweet. But she didn't belong here."

"But *I* do."

"This is your *home*, baby. It may not be perfect—no one's is. Not even Meagan's. But it's where you come from. You can't change that."

Bobby raised a hand to the back of his neck and drew a deep burned-out breath, all the fight draining out of him. As much as he didn't want it to be the case, his mom was right. He loved Meagan so much he ached with it sometimes. Especially now. She made him want all the things that a man like him had no right to; marriage, kids, and all the trappings. But they were from totally different worlds. He would just have to resign himself to the fact that he'd never have those things. He loved Meagan and Jay too much to endanger them in any way. And if he wasn't going to have that life with them, he'd just as soon not have it at all.

ॐ

Five days had passed since she'd last seen Bobby.

Meagan rolled over onto her side and glanced at the clock on her bedside table. She groaned. 12:30. Her eyes wouldn't even stay closed. But that was just as well. When she did press them shut all she could see was him.

She rolled onto her back and pressed the heels of her palms to her eyes. She *had* to get more sleep. This evening she'd snapped at Jay several times for things that ordinarily wouldn't bother her in the least. But she'd been so tired. She'd hardly slept since the night before the funeral, and now she was back at work, on her feet all day trying to make up for the appointments she'd cancelled last week.

With a sigh she dropped hands to her sides. Then she kicked off the covers and swung her legs over the side of the bed. This was pointless. She could at least be watching the Home Shopping Network, or some old movie. She'd had better luck falling asleep on the couch these past few nights, anyway. Why she even bothered going to bed was beyond her.

The thick nighttime silence stirred to life suddenly when the phone beside her bed rang. Meagan started and her pulse quickened, the same way it did every time the phone had rung these past several days, although there was something alarming about the sound this late at night.

It rang again, and she snatched up the receiver.

"Hello?" Her voice sounded breathless.

No reply came over the line, but it wasn't dead, either. Someone was there. Tears rose from their seemingly endless supply.

"Bobby?" She clutched the phone with both hands, as if it could give her some kind of hold on him.

Still, for a long moment, no reply came. Then she heard the slow intake of a breath. "It's me. Sorry to call so late. It's just...I just..."

His deep voice sounded haggard, strained, and she longed to be able to sooth his hurt with her touch. "Are you OK?"

"Yeah. I'm fine." There was a long silence. "I'm at my mother's place."

Meagan looked down at her knees. "I know. I

called your store. Todd told me."

Another long silence.

Why didn't you tell me! How could you just leave without a word? She wanted to yell. She wanted to break down sobbing.

"When will you be coming home?"

He took a breath. "I'll probably leave here Saturday morning. So I should be back in Lubbock sometime Saturday afternoon."

"And you'll come over when you get back?" She couldn't help the timidity in her voice. She squeezed her eyes shut, afraid of what his answer would be.

He stammered a little. "I...I just don't think that's such a good idea."

Tears began to fall. She knew her voice would quiver with the next words she spoke, but she needed a definitive answer. "Is it over between us?"

Again he stammered. "I...ah, Meagan, we just can't...I just don't see how..." He paused, remaining silent for such a long, terminal moment that she could barely contain a sob. "Yeah," he said at last. "Yeah, it is."

She did sob then and sniffed, reaching for a tissue from her night stand.

"Don't cry, baby."

"Don't you tell me not to cry, Bobby Kerr!" She snapped the words at him through her constricted throat. "I imagine it doesn't make it any easier for you to do this with me sitting here cryin' into the phone. But you're gonna hear it." She sniffed again, the tears giving way to all the anger she'd tried to produce over the past week. "You're just gonna have to sit and listen to my heart breaking because of you. I love you, Bobby. And you love me. I know you do. And this makes no sense."

"It's the only way that makes sense." He broke in. "We are worlds apart, Meagan. I can't ask you to commit yourself and Jay to me—a man like me."

"Give me a break!" She almost shouted into the receiver. "Do you think you're the only person in this world with a hateful family? Do you think you're the only recovering alcoholic? Or the only man who's ever..." She stopped short. What was she doing? What was the point?

"Who's ever what?" His voice sounded sharp. "Hit a woman? Shoved, slapped, punched, beat up a woman?"

Meagan wiped her eyes and nose with her tissue, and took a deep, steadying breath.

"What if I do that to you some day? It's just not a chance I want to take." His words sounded firm. But there was something about his tone, something unsure. Like he wanted her to talk him out of it. Like he just needed to be convinced.

"I'm willing to." She seized her opportunity to drive a wedge in the open door. "*I'm* willing to take that risk. Doesn't that mean anything?"

"I know what you think," he said. "You think it won't ever happen to you. You think I'd never hurt you. And I'd rather die, Meagan. I really would. *I'd rather die* than hurt you or Jay. But this is what I am."

"That's a lie! It's what everyone back there—*back home*—keeps telling you. And you keep believing it. But I am not stupid. I am not just blindly in love with you. I have talked to Audrey. I've met your family. I know where you come from. And I know who you are." Her anger subsided as the all too familiar heartache took its place. "You're a good Christian man now. A new man. And I want you to be my husband."

She drew in a long breath and clutched the receiver with both hands. She was desperate to convince him. But it wasn't up to her. And even if she could, his confidence would only last until his next trip home. It had to come from somewhere other than her.

Lord, help him. Show him who he is now, who You've made him.

She took another deep breath and said the next words that came to her mind. "But I *do* have a child to think about, and what I won't have is a man who's around some and then gone some, around and then gone again, depending on how he *feels* about himself."

She paused. They were back to silence again.

"So take it back, Bobby." Her voice cracked and she sighed. "You said it was over between us. Just take it back and come on home. If you don't, it really *will* be over between us."

Meagan listened as the silence coming over the line grew louder and louder. She could hang on all night, waiting for him to say he was wrong, and he was headed home to her. But he had been deceived; by his family, by himself, by the Devil. She took a deep breath, squared her shoulders, and dried her eyes.

"Goodbye, Bobby."

14

Bobby had been back in Lubbock for two weeks.

Working from opening until closing every day had done nothing to fill the void left by Meagan's absence from his life. It had done nothing to silence the sound of her goodbye the last time he'd spoken with her. If anything it made his loneliness worse.

He tossed his pen down onto the desk and leaned back in his chair. A glance at his watch told him it was nearly six. Tonight he would break this new habit of working extra late hours. He'd go home at a regular time. He'd microwave some dinner and watch some television. He'd go to bed by eleven. He'd go back to his life before her. He had to; otherwise he'd probably go crazy.

With a heavy sigh he picked up a small stack of invoices and gave them a tap on the desk to straighten them. When he'd laid them aside his glance wandered to the phone. Several times a day, every day, since the last time he'd talked to her he'd fought this battle. His fingers itched to pick up the phone and call her the same way they used to itch to pick up a beer to dull his mind. The latter battle he'd won recently. If his last trip back home couldn't drive him to drink again, he'd probably do OK. But the more he thought about his decision to break it off with Meagan, the more he thought he was wrong. And each time he looked at a telephone he came closer to picking it up and making the call.

Do it.

Tight knots began to form in his stomach, and he glanced at his hand which had, at some point, come to rest on the receiver. He took a breath and shook his head. No. It was too much to hope that the Lord would be telling him it was OK to call her. She'd made her position very clear last time they'd talked. She wouldn't take a chance on a man who she thought wasn't ready to commit his whole heart and life to her and Jay. She didn't want a man she couldn't trust to stick with her, regardless of his own crisis of self-confidence.

As much as he wanted to commit his whole heart and life to her, he'd probably never feel worthy of her love and trust. He'd never trust himself to be good to her. So he might as well just get used to the idea. But he died a little bit every day when he remembered how she'd told him she wanted him to be her husband. When he thought of how that's exactly what he wanted to be. But mostly when he thought about how such a situation would ultimately never work out.

He drew his hand away from the phone.

Despite what Meagan wanted to believe about him, and despite what Brent kept telling him, he was what he was. An alcoholic. An abuser.

A new creation. A child of God.

He shook his head to try and clear the idea away. *Maybe. But still....*God had saved him. *Thank you, Lord, for that.* But that was all the more reason not to put others in his dangerous path. He was obligated not to.

No. He swiveled the chair around to the computer. He'd go home. Get back to life as he used to know it.

That was the best plan. As he reached for the mouse to shut the computer down, the little electronic chime sounded. New email.

The message was from Brent, who had spent the better part of last week trying to convince him to leave the small world of his hometown behind for good.

Bobby grinned. Leave it to Brent to get the last word in.

"Go home to her." Those had been Brent's last words to him before he got on the road back to Lubbock.

Go home to her.

He opened the message. All it contained was a passage of scripture:

"For I know the plans I have for you," declares the Lord, "plans to prosper you and not to harm you, plans to give you hope and a future."

A future and a family.

Silent, stoic tears welled up and spilled over before Bobby even had the chance to tamp them back down again. *Hope and a future.* Even on the day he was saved he hadn't believed he was entitled to that much. It had been more than enough that God had forgiven him every evil thing he'd ever done. He hadn't felt right asking for more. And yet God was offering more. Wasn't He?

The uncertainty of the revelation almost made him slide out of his chair and onto his knees. *Just tell me, Lord. Just tell me what to do? Is this You? Or is it me?* He swallowed hard and took a deep breath, shuffling through his desk drawers. He had a box of tissues somewhere, and he couldn't walk out of this office looking as if he'd been bawling like a baby.

Irritation mounted with each drawer he pulled

out, with each item he pushed aside. It must be his own selfish desire making him think that calling Meagan and taking back everything he said last time he talked to her was God's plan. No. This was life. Sure, he wanted her. But people didn't always get what they wanted, and sitting here dwelling on it, crying about it, wouldn't change a thing. *Time to move on and get over it.*

For I know the plans I have for you, plans to prosper you and not to harm you, plans to give you hope and a future.

Bobby's hands stilled and his shoulders sagged, his resistance melting like wax about to be poured into a new mold. He leaned forward, resting his elbows on his desk, burying his face in his hands.

Lord, could it be possible? Could it really be possible?

Bobby held his breath and closed his eyes. He had to hear for sure. Otherwise he'd assume it was his own heart speaking, and not God's will. But he heard it again. The still small voice, comforting, promising hope and a future.

Go home to her.

Bobby laughed out loud and spun his chair around. He didn't try to stifle it. Let anyone passing by his office think he'd gone insane, he didn't care. He laughed as he shut down his computer, as he crossed the room to turn the overhead lights off. He locked and closed his office door, heading across the hard concrete floor of the store.

He raised one hand and ruffled his hair, unable to contain a giddy, probably goofy looking grin. He was going home to her. Granted, she may not throw herself into his arms when she saw him, but he could convince her. He *would* convince her. Whatever it took, that's what he'd do. He just had one stop to make first.

❧∽

"Thanks for being here, Caroline. I just don't think I could get through this alone." Meagan glanced at the clock on her microwave as she poured a pot of freshly brewed tea into a pitcher. "Besides which, it'll be good to have a witness."

"Why are you so nervous?" Caroline pulled a small stack of plates out of a cabinet and turned toward the kitchen table.

"I'm not nervous." Meagan glanced at her sister who turned and gave her an *Oh, please!* look. "OK. I'm a little nervous. I have no idea why." She turned back to her tea preparation. "I lived with the man for five years. We both know the good, the bad, and the ugly about each other. It's not like I want him back. It's not like I need to make a good impression." She finished stirring the tea, then rinsed the wooden spoon and set it in the sink. She rubbed her hands together. "Is it cold in here?"

Caroline shook her head.

"My hands are freezing."

"Calm down."

"What if he wants to take Jay from me? What if he wants to work out some kind of joint custody arrangement where he has Jay half the year or something like that?"

"I thought y'all worked all that out in the divorce settlement."

"But what if he's changed his mind?" She wrung her hands. She could feel hysteria beginning to lodge itself in her chest. She took a deep breath. "What if he tries to take Jay from me?"

"Meagan, calm down." The sound of her sister's voice soothed her nerves a little. This was why she'd wanted Caroline here. Carefree as she usually seemed, Caroline could always be counted on for calm, rational support in an emergency. "If he's changed his mind about anything, it's you. Maybe he wants *you* back."

She frowned. *No. Surely not.* In order for him to get her back, he'd have to take Jay, too. But Kevin didn't want a family. Did he? He'd never wanted a family. In all the years she'd known him, he never even conceded that *maybe someday* he'd want kids. In fact, he'd been very vociferously against the idea. She hadn't even been able to stop and admire someone's baby at the grocery store without him making some acerbic comment about not getting any ideas.

But people changed. And if he'd changed his mind, and now he wanted Jay, maybe he wanted her back, too. Maybe he realized his mistake in leaving her. Maybe he'd had some kind of soul searching experience out in the desert and he'd decided he wanted his family back.

"I hadn't thought about that." But thinking about it now made her ears start to ring and her vision blur.

"I'm teasing!" Caroline groaned. "Pull yourself together. Kevin wants to see Jay. He wants to see his son. That's it. And you know what? Maybe the reality of it will motivate him to send you a little child support."

"Or maybe the reality of it will motivate him to start making demands."

Caroline opened her mouth to speak, but stopped short when the doorbell rang.

Meagan almost gasped as she reached out to

clutch her sister's hands. "It's him."

"Dang, girl! Your hands are *freezing*! Take a breath."

Meagan did as her sister instructed. She took one deep breath, and then another. It didn't really help.

"You want me to get the door?" Caroline rubbed her hands briskly, looking like she thought Meagan might collapse at any second.

"No." Another deep breath. "No. I can do this. I just wish Bobby was here."

"Meagan—"

"I know, I know." She held up her hands in mock surrender. "I know."

The doorbell rang again and Jay stirred from his place on the couch.

"I guess I better get it before Jay does." She followed Jay to the door, pausing, trying to still her trembling, clammy hand by squeezing the doorknob. *Enough!* She took a determined breath, turned the knob, and opened the door.

Meagan had not deluded herself regarding how unprepared she was for this meeting. If there was one thing she knew for sure, it was how not ready she was to see her ex husband again after more than three years. She saw the same mentality reflected in Kevin's expression. He was apparently just as unprepared.

Say something! Her thoughts spun furiously. *Invite him in. Ask him how he's been. Introduce him to his son.* She didn't know what to say first, so she stood as if dumbstruck, staring at him where he stood on her front porch holding a pizza box.

Kevin cleared his throat. "Wow! Meagan. You look great. The last time I saw you, you were..."

"Seven months pregnant." She finished the

thought for him. Her voice was soft and shaky, and she felt tears threaten. It had been at the lawyer's office as they worked out the details of their divorce. That had been the last time she'd seen him. She'd been so scared. She wanted to fall to her knees and beg him not to leave her. And here he was looking back at her with those same crystal clear blue eyes, with the same short brown hair, the same straight perfect smile. He hadn't changed a bit since the day he abandoned her.

He looked down. "Um... yeah."

Jay had shifted into his shy mode. He hid behind her skirt, reaching around timidly to peek at the stranger who he must be thinking was the pizza delivery guy.

She took another deep breath. "Well, come on in." Pulling the door open wider, she stepped aside, guiding Jay out of the way. Kevin handed her the pizza box as he crossed the threshold. He stopped short in the middle of the room.

"Oh. Hi, Caroline," he said. "I didn't know you'd be here."

"Hi, Kevin. How've you been?"

Meagan slipped passed them to put the pizza on the table. Jay followed right on her heels. As soon as her hands were free he held up his arms to be picked up. She settled him awkwardly on her hip. He'd probably grown an inch in the last month or so, and was really getting too big and heavy for her to carry him around much anymore. But the way he clung to her now and buried his little face in her neck whenever Kevin glanced at him gave her a small measure of comfort.

"So, did you finish up at UT yet?" Kevin asked Caroline.

"I've got one more year, and I'll be done with my Master's program."

"Master's program. Wow!" Kevin's eyebrows shot up, making him look appropriately impressed. Then he grinned.

Oh, how Meagan wished he hadn't grinned like that! He'd grinned just like that on the day she'd met him, and the day he'd proposed, and a thousand other times—good times. It made it almost impossible for her to keep thinking of him as the villain. "I remember you all dressed up for your little senior prom, with your sparkly dress and your fancy hairdo. Now you're probably smarter than me."

Caroline's demeanor softened a little and she smiled mischievously. "What do you mean 'now'?"

Kevin's grin widened, and he relaxed. Then he turned his attention back to Meagan, his gaze ultimately locking onto Jay, and remaining there for a long, awkward moment.

"Um, this is Jay."

Kevin took a step or two closer. "Hi, Jay."

Jay turned his head away and locked his arms around Meagan's neck. After a moment he peeked back at the man standing in the middle of his house.

"My name's Kevin. I brought you some pizza. Do you like pizza?"

Jay glanced at the table and then back at Kevin. Then he smiled shyly and nodded.

"Oh, *good*." Kevin exaggerated his relief. "I was afraid you wouldn't like it. Then I might have to eat it all."

Jay began squirming—his signal that he was OK to be put down now. He hit the floor and started hopping around, chanting "Pizza! Pizza! Pizza!"

"Does he know who I am?" Kevin spoke quietly.

Panic flared. Meagan reached out to grab the back of a chair with one hand. "He's only just met you."

"I know." Kevin said quickly. "I just wondered if you had told him about me."

She gritted her teeth as Caroline moved past her and started filling glasses with ice. "He's only three. It hasn't come up. And since you weren't around and didn't seem the least bit interested, I didn't think it was necessary to confuse him."

Kevin looked down. "I didn't come here to fight, Meagan. I just wanted to see y'all." He reached for his wallet, separating the bill compartments and pulling out a small slip of paper. "I brought you something."

Meagan took the offered paper and unfolded it. It was a check for five hundred dollars. She tried to blink away the tears that suddenly filled her eyes. "Thanks. I guess I can forward it to one of the collection agencies."

She thought she saw him wince, and she had to bite back an apology. She wasn't sorry. He ought to at least know what she'd end up having to do with the money. It wouldn't cover close to everything he owed, but a small payment would get at least one of them off her back for awhile.

"No, Meagan. That money's for you and Jay."

She gave an exasperated sigh. "Kevin—"

He held up a hand to quiet her. "Just listen. I didn't have a job. I'd been without a job for two years without any prospects that would pay many bills. I thought filing for bankruptcy was the only way I'd get by. I never intended to stick you with those debts."

That much was true. Kevin may have been thoughtless and irresponsible. But he wasn't downright mean. Meagan folded her arms across her chest and watched him shift his weight awkwardly from one foot to the other under her level stare.

"But I found a job. A good one. At a newspaper in Cheyenne."

Her jaw wanted to drop, but she held it firmly in place. "Wyoming?"

He nodded. "I've talked with the collection agencies. I've worked it out with them. They shouldn't be calling you anymore. I'll try to send a little money each month. But I'm not sure exactly how all the finances are going to work out until I get there." He glanced away for a second, then met her gaze again. "I'm sorry, Meagan. I never meant to make things harder on you."

A slow smile stole its way out of her heart, followed by a hoarse, joyful laugh. It was all she could do to keep from throwing her arms around his neck and bursting into tears. He had taken care of the debt collector situation, and was now promising to send her child support on top of that. She stood staring at him for a moment, letting it sink in.

"Oh, Kevin," she whispered. "I could just kiss you!" She gave in to her earlier temptation and did throw her arms around his neck, laughing out loud. It took just a minute, but then she felt his arms close around her warmly. She looked up into his smiling face. "Oh, thank you."

Hold it! What was that look she saw there in his eyes? That penetratingly intimate look she'd seen countless times in better days, as his gaze took in every line of her face, settling finally on her mouth. Her smile faded. He wanted to kiss her. If they were alone now, he would.

"Whoa, now." The sound of Caroline's voice apparently broke the spell that had entranced him. He blinked and looked away. "Let's not get carried away."

Meagan pushed herself out of his arms, but she could suppress neither the sense of freedom she suddenly felt, nor her smile. She and Jay were going to be OK. This was a sign from God if ever there was one. They'd be all right. God was taking care of them.

She may not have Bobby anymore. The thought sobered her and she felt her smile fade. *They* may not have been meant to be. But her finances were about to improve, and a major stressor had been relieved—hopefully for good.

She took Kevin's arm and led him to her kitchen table, where Caroline had already helped Jay into his booster chair and seated herself. "Let's have some pizza."

☙❧

Something was going on. Bobby turned off the engine and pulled his keys from the ignition. That was Caroline's car in the driveway behind Meagan's. But the pickup with New Mexico plates, the one he'd just parked behind on the curb, he didn't know whose that was.

Who did Meagan know in New Mexico?

Once she'd mentioned having some relatives over in Clovis. Maybe they were in town for a visit.

Whatever. It didn't matter. Bobby opened his door and stepped out of his truck. He'd get down on both knees in front of every distant relative she had in Texas and New Mexico if that's what it took to make her believe him.

Purposeful strides carried him to her front door. He raised a hand to ring the bell, but a high pitched, very excited squeal pierced the dusky evening air stopping him. Bobby grinned. Jay sounded very happy about something. His outburst was followed immediately by adult laughter and boisterous conversation.

Bobby ran a hand through his hair, checked his shirt tail, and straightened the collar of his white button down work shirt. Maybe he should go home and change. Put on a nicer pair of jeans, and maybe a fresh shirt.

Don't be stupid. He grinned wider. She wasn't going to say no because he had his work shirt on.

But what if she did say no? What if she'd made her mind up and he couldn't change it?

He pulled the little ring box he'd just obtained at the mall out of his pocket and opened it. It wasn't a very big diamond. But it was what he could afford. What if she wouldn't let him put it on her finger?

What had happened to the resolve he'd felt a couple of hours ago? What had happened to all his confidence?

Lord, help me.

Bobby stuffed the little ring box back into his pocket, swallowed hard and took a deep breath. Then he raised his hand and rang the bell.

∽∾

"Oh, boy." Meagan sighed and shook her head, watching her son bouncing around the room like a monkey in a cage. He was wired from all the food and attention. "I'm never gonna be able to bring this boy down enough to put him to bed."

Jay stood up straight in the middle of the room, filled his lungs and opened his mouth to let out another shout.

"Jay!" Meagan's tone was sharp, and Jay shut his mouth, turning to look at her with an impish little grin. "Use your inside voice, please."

He took another breath and opened his mouth again, but was silenced by the sound of the doorbell.

"Ooh." Caroline crooned. "Saved by the bell."

Meagan rolled her eyes and groaned at the joke as she rose to answer the door. Jay hopped along behind her, running right into her when she stopped to pull the door open. "Oh! Careful, honey." She let the door swing open on its own and bent down to catch him before he fell backwards.

The voice that greeted her from across the threshold was soft, deep, warm, and the endearment it spoke, painfully familiar.

"Hi, baby."

15

Before Meagan could even straighten up and turn around, Jay let out an earsplitting squeal.

"Bobby! Bobby!" Jay bolted out onto the porch and held his arms up, jumping up and down in place as if that could make the man standing there pick him up more quickly.

Meagan kept her gaze fastened on her child, afraid to raise it to Bobby's face. But his strong hands—the same ones which had touched her so intimately the last time she'd seen him—reached down to fulfill Jay's demand, picking him up and pulling her gaze up, too.

It was really him. Meagan didn't know whether to smile, or laugh, or cry, or snatch Jay from his arms and slam the door in his face.

No. That wouldn't work. Jay had already seen him. Jay had already locked his little arms around Bobby's neck and given him a sloppy kiss hello.

Meagan's heart completely melted at the sight, and she had to fight to keep hold on the last waning scraps of her composure. She wanted to do the same. She wanted to throw herself into his arms and tell him everything that had happened tonight; that Kevin wasn't interested in taking Jay from her, that he'd worked out an arrangement with his creditors who would stop calling her, that he'd promised to start paying child support. Now he was standing on her front porch, and that could only mean that he missed her these past few weeks.

She felt a sudden check in her spirit. Missing her didn't mean he intended to come back to her permanently, and she would not have him any other way. And he couldn't just drop by when the mood struck him. He couldn't do that to Jay.

When Bobby turned his warm, happy gaze to her, she folded her arms across her chest. "You should have called."

His smile faded and he had the decency to look ashamed. "I know." He glanced down and shifted Jay's weight in his arms. "I thought about it, but I...Baby, I just wanted to talk to you—face to face."

"You should have called. You can't just drop by, Bobby. Jay is too attached to you. If it's not gonna work out between—"

"Meagan." The warmth of his voice reached out and touched her almost physically. "I'd really like to talk to you. It's important."

She sighed and dropped arms to her sides. He was already here. Jay had already seen him. He might as well come in and spend a little time with the boy who'd been asking about him every day for three weeks. She stepped aside so he could come in.

His presence charged the room as he carried Jay past her. Meagan took a deep breath and closed the door, leaning on it briefly for the sense of strength and stability the feel of the hard wooden surface instilled. It wasn't moving, and neither would she.

When she turned back around she found Bobby, stopped in his tracks, standing in the middle of the room. His gaze had locked curiously on Kevin.

Oh, boy. If anything could try his temper to the

breaking point, it would probably be this. Meagan took a deep breath and plunged into the introduction. If there was going to be an ugly confrontation, she'd just as soon get it over with.

"Bobby, this is Kevin Layne. My ex husband."

Bobby tensed. Probably no one else noticed, but Meagan saw it. The lines of his face hardened, his eyes narrowed, his jaw clamped shut, his hold on Jay tightened ever so slightly. She watched as his gaze covered every inch of Kevin's tall frame, from his face all the way down to his boots and then back up again.

"Kevin..." Meagan paused and swallowed. "This is Bobby Kerr." *My what?* She'd introduced Kevin as her ex husband. Not long ago she might have introduced Bobby as her future husband. Or at least her boyfriend. But what was he to her now? She didn't know, so she left it at that. Nothing.

Still the two men stood, each sizing the other up.

Finally, after what felt like an eternity, Kevin extended his hand. Another eternity passed, and then Bobby returned the gesture.

"Pleased to meet you," Kevin said evenly.

Bobby responded with a curt nod as Jay held out his arms to Meagan. She took him from Bobby's grasp and then took a few steps backward.

"Um...Bobby, there's some pizza here if you're hungry."

"Meagan, I really should get going." Kevin turned to her. "Thanks for letting me come by." Then to her sister. "Caroline, it was good to see you again."

Meagan cast a sly glance at Bobby to find him staring at the floor. She clutched Jay to her side and slipped past him. "We'll walk you out."

"No! No!" Jay's high pitched protest rang in

Meagan's ear as he twisted in her arms and reached over her shoulder in Bobby's direction.

"We'll be right back," she assured him before pulling the front door closed behind her. Silently she followed Kevin down the front walk to his truck. He turned to her when they got there.

"Jay, can you tell Kevin thank you for the pizza?"

Jay smiled. "Thank you."

"You're welcome, Jay." He shot a quick glance at Meagan before returning it to his son. "I hope I get to see you again sometime."

Jay nodded.

Meagan put him down and he trotted toward the front porch. "You stay on the porch or in the grass, you hear?"

"OK, Mama."

She turned back to Kevin to find him studying her closely.

"So, is that your boyfriend in there?"

She shook her head. "Not as of a couple of weeks ago."

Kevin nodded and glanced back at the house. "You sure?"

"I guess."

"Jay sure seems to like him."

She shrugged and looked toward Jay. She couldn't maintain eye contact with Kevin. He had a look in his eyes that was making her increasingly uncomfortable. Like he had feelings for her he was about to reveal. She didn't want to hear it.

"Are you gonna tell Jay about me someday?"

She let the air out of her lungs in a long, sorrowful sigh. "I guess one of these days he's gonna want to know. So, yeah, I'll tell him."

There was so much else he wanted to say. She could see it all right there in his eyes, plain as the day was long. He regretted leaving them.

Not too many years ago, in one of her "then-he'll-be-sorry" fantasies, she'd pictured this moment. She'd imagined him coming back to town and visiting her in her cozy little home, with their precious son. In her daydream he'd fallen to his knees in tears, begging her forgiveness, telling her how empty his life was, swearing he still loved her, begging her to take him back. In her daydream she'd stood her ground proudly and coolly, unmoved by his remorse, yet immensely satisfied at his expression of it.

In real life, however, standing here next to him, in the flesh, his repentance obvious by everything he'd said and done tonight, the situation was not so fulfilling. She glanced back at him. His gaze had settled on Jay who sat poking a stick at some poor bug on the front porch.

"He looks like me." The quiet awe in Kevin's voice brought the sudden sting of tears and an unexpected sob. She pressed a hand to her mouth and got herself under control—just barely.

"Yes." Her voice was little more than a whisper. "He does."

"It just wasn't real to me, Meagan. I mean, I knew you were pregnant. But it just didn't seem real. And I don't know what my problem was. I should have turned around and come right back home." He paused, shook his head and glanced back up at the house again. "No. I should have never left..."

She almost choked on a sob. "Please don't—"

He held up one hand to quiet her, then he shook his head. "I won't. You've got a nice, orderly life now. I didn't come here to work my way back into it. I know we still don't see eye to eye on the whole God thing, and that's important to you. But I still love you, Meagan. I didn't realize it until you opened that front door and stood there looking me in the eyes. But it's true."

"Bobby, please..." The breath caught in her throat. *Oh, Lord, please say I didn't really just call him by Bobby's name.* But she had. She could tell by the sudden look of revelation on his face.

"Oh, I see." He gave her a smile she couldn't quite read. "Like *that*, is it?"

"Kevin, I'm sorry..."

He reached for her and pulled her into an embrace. "No. *I'm* sorry. For everything. I promise I'll do what I can to help from now on."

Meagan slid her arms around his waist and leaned on him for a long moment, feeling the years of anger and hostility melt away as forgiveness seemed to wash her soul.

"Listen." His voice was soft and low against her hair. "About Bobby...if y'all should get married...would he be a good father to Jay?"

Meagan squeezed her eyes shut, sending a wash of tears down her cheeks. "Yes." She nodded. "He would be a great father."

Finally, Kevin gently set her an arm's length away from him.

"I guess I should hit the road. I was planning on getting back to Santa Fe tonight." He pulled open the door of his beat up old truck. The same one he'd had when they'd been married. The same one he'd bought new when they'd been in college.

"You think this old thing'll get you all the way to

Wyoming?"

He stepped up into the cab and slid behind the wheel, pulling the door shut with a hollow sounding thud. He draped one arm outside the open window and patted the door. "I guess it'll have to."

"Let me know how things go, OK?"

He nodded and grinned. "I will. I'll give you a call when I get settled." He started the engine and put the truck in gear. "Now, you go on inside and work it out with him. It only took him a couple of weeks to come back. He obviously has more sense than I ever did."

He gave her a wink and a wave, then he pulled away from the curb. She watched his truck as it retreated up the street, turned the corner, and disappeared.

Meagan wiped her tears away and folded her arms across her chest, taking a deep breath of dry, west Texas air. So far this evening hadn't gone anything like she'd expected. And it wasn't nearly over yet.

∾❦

Bobby didn't know how to react.

When he saw Kevin take her into his arms, his grip on the curtain he'd drawn back grew so tight, it occurred to him he might actually, inadvertently pull the rod down. He expelled a frustrated breath and loosened his hold on the fabric.

What was he supposed to make of all this? He'd come here tonight intending to propose, and now she was standing on her front curb in her ex-husband's arms. Still! She was *still* standing there in his arms. This was no quick "keep-in-touch" farewell hug. She was *still* standing there with his arms tight around her, and hers around him.

He tossed the curtain aside, on the verge of storming out the front door and dragging her back inside. Yes! That's *exactly* what he'd do. He'd drag her back inside, then kiss her so soundly she wouldn't remember her own name, let alone Kevin Layne's. He'd remind her in no uncertain terms that not too many nights ago *she* had invited *him* to spend the night here with her, that she had *begged* him not to leave. Bobby turned, intent on doing just that, but stopped short when he almost ran right into Caroline.

"I...I..." He stammered, shoving a frustrated hand through his hair. "I was under the impression that he wasn't interested in...in..."

Caroline's eyebrows shot up. "Yeah, well, I was under the impression that you felt the same way. And so was she. Funny how that's usually the impression a girl gets when a man dumps her."

Bobby opened his mouth to respond, but he couldn't think of a single way to answer, and the sound of a slamming door outside diverted his attention, anyway. He turned and pulled back the curtain again in time to see Kevin pull away from the curb. Without Meagan. Bobby breathed a sigh of relief and all the fight drained right out of him.

"How much does she hate me?" He didn't turn around. "I bought a ring today. I came here to beg her to take me back. Do I even stand a chance?"

Bobby started at the feel of Caroline's hand on his shoulder.

"She doesn't hate you." Her voice was soft, like she really *was* on his side. The thought bolstered his sagging confidence. "And I think you have a fair chance. Now." Her tone brightened as she turned and headed back to the kitchen. "How about some pizza. Nourishment for the coming battle."

"No, thanks." He let the panel fall back into place. "Tea?"

He shook his head. It was too late, anyway. He heard the front door open and then Jay bounded into the room and wrapped his little arms around his legs.

❧◆❧

Nope. This night wasn't anywhere near over.

"Whoa, there." Bobby's smile looked so heartfelt when he looked down at Jay, ruffling the boy's hair with one hand, that it brought a reluctant smile to Meagan's own face. When he raised his gaze to hers, however, she put on the stoniest expression she could summon. She glared at him, then she turned and headed for the kitchen to clear the table.

Caroline stood regarding her with one raised eyebrow. "Come on, Meagan," she whispered. "Can't you see how sorry he is? Cut him some slack."

"Don't you *even* take his side!" Meagan pushed the clipped, harsh whispered words out through gritted teeth.

"Believe it or not, I'm on *your* side."

She shot Caroline what she hoped was a skeptical look.

"I *am*." Caroline's astonished chuckle sounded far too confident. "You told me you thought he was 'the one,' did you not?"

Meagan narrowed her eyes furiously, but then admitted to it. "I did."

"Well, now he's here. I don't know what his problem was, but he came back. And I think what he's got to say, you just might want to hear."

She stole a glance around the corner to find Bobby sitting on the couch with Jay chatting happily on his lap.

"I'll go give Jay his bath and try to calm him down a little." Caroline's voice drew her attention.

Meagan gave a doubtful grunt. "Good luck."

"Talk to him." Her sister demanded her attention with a gentle hand on her arm. She sounded so earnest, almost like she was pleading Bobby's case for him. "Try to work it out with him. You might not get another chance."

She followed Caroline to the edge of the living room.

"Time for your bath, Jay."

"No! No bath!"

Caroline reached down to pick her nephew up only to have him start whining and wiggling to get away. Then the tears started. Jay reached out to Bobby pitifully.

"I'll tell you what." Caroline said. "I'll give you your bath and maybe we'll read a few stories. Then, if you're good, maybe Bobby can come tuck you into bed. How does that sound?"

Jay sniffed a few times and swiped at his tearful eyes. Then he nodded. "OK." His little voice sounded so miserable. But Aunt Caroline's bargain must have seemed agreeable to him, because he went without further protest. Meagan even heard a little giggle come from the direction of the bathroom once they made it that far.

Bobby stirred from his seat and began to cross the room. She turned her back and retreated into the kitchen.

The last time he'd been in her house she'd made herself more vulnerable than she'd been to any man in years, and he'd walked out despite her pleas for him to stay. If he had something to say to her, she would definitely not make it easy for him. He was going to have to open his heart up the same way she had.

She transferred the leftover pizza into a zipper storage bag, and grabbed the pitcher of tea, crossing to put both into the refrigerator.

"So, um...what did your ex want?"

Something inside her snapped at the question. She couldn't name it, but she felt it snap like a brittle little twig under a giant's foot. She slammed the refrigerator door hard enough that jars rattled inside. "Don't start!" She almost yelled the words. "Don't you dare start asking me questions like that. The last word I got from you was that it was over between us. What goes on in my life doesn't concern you anymore."

Bobby opened his mouth as if to respond, but whatever retort had formed in his mind died after a few seconds of meeting her level, angry stare. With an exasperated sounding sigh he turned and began stacking the plates, then carrying them to the sink.

"Meagan." He followed her back to the table. "I didn't come here to fight with you."

"Well, that's just too bad." She turned and thrust empty tea glasses into his hands. "Because you've got one coming. You've got at least one big, angry, screaming fight coming to you after the way you treated me last time you were here."

He put the glasses down with such force that she was surprised when they didn't break. Then he spun to face her. "Now hold on just a minute. I could have treated you a *whole lot* worse."

"And just what is *that* supposed to mean?" She lowered her voice, but it did little to curb the vehemence behind her words. "You think just because you didn't go through with using me—even though you thought about it—that I'm going to find you somehow noble? And then you just dump me! Because you just don't see how it could work out between us. Because you can't ask me to commit my life to 'a man like you.'"

"I didn't use you."

"Well, thank you for that." She turned and slapped a dishrag down onto the table and began scrubbing.

"I never thought about using you." His tone was low and gentle. Remorseful. "Even if we'd gone through with it, that's not what it would have been. Not to me. And I should have never called and broke it off with you. I should have never gone back to Blithe Settlement after the funeral. You were right about that. I don't know what I was thinking, Meagan."

She finished wiping down the table and turned to face him. What he said was true. She knew it was. There had never been any doubt in her mind about his feelings for her. That last night they were together he had been just as carried away, whether by a tide of emotion, or stress, or whatever. Looking at him now, at his guileless expression, pleading with her to believe him, only confirmed that belief.

But she was still so angry she could spit, and she didn't know what she wanted him to do or say to make it up to her.

"What do you want, Bobby?" She finally managed to ask, her toned controlled, but still cold. "Why are you here?"

He took an incredibly deep breath and held it for a long, long moment. *Let it out,* she wanted to say. *Let it out before you pass out.* He looked like passing out was exactly what he was about to do. The color drained from his face. Then he reached into his front pocket and pulled out a small box.

A ring box.

His hands shook as he opened it and turned it for her inspection. "I...I..." He stammered and then stalled.

Meagan pressed one hand to her mouth to try and stop the sudden, hot flow of tears that rushed up as she looked at the ring, hardly even seeing it. When she raised her gaze to his face he tried to smile, but it did little to disguise the terror in his eyes.

So what scares you more? She wanted to ask. *The idea of me saying no? Or the idea of me saying yes?*

"What do you expect me to do, Bobby?" The words came out as a hoarse, barely controlled whisper. "Do you expect me to throw myself into your arms?"

"Yes!" He almost yelled. "Yes. That's exactly what I expect you to do. Because I love you, and you love me. I know you do. And this—me putting this ring on your finger, and you throwing yourself into my arms, and us getting married as soon as possible—this makes sense. Besides God, it's the only thing in my whole screwed up life that's *ever* made any sense."

"Yes, but for how long will you feel that way?" She took a step or two back. "Until the wedding, when your family shows up and you think about how rotten your life was before, and how nobody can trust you, and how you can't expose me and Jay to all that? At which point, what will you do? Leave me standing at the altar?"

"Baby, I will feel this way for the rest of my life.

God has promised me hope and a future, and you're it. You and Jay. I'll never leave you. Not at the altar. Not ever. And if you're worried about the affect seeing my family might have on me, we won't invite them to the wedding. We'll never see them again." He countered her steps backward by taking a few of his own in her direction. "Please. I'm askin' you to trust me. Marry me, and let me prove it to you."

She couldn't do anything but stare at him. *Lord, I want to believe him. I want to say 'yes.' More than anything. Could this really be possible? What should I do? He said he'd never leave me, God. But I've heard that before. And he's already left me once.*

"Um, excuse me." She started at the sound of Caroline's voice. "As much as I hate to interrupt a good knock-down-drag-out, or standoff, or whatever's going on here, Jay's getting impatient. He's had his bath and his story, and he won't wait any longer for Bobby to come tuck him in."

Bobby took a breath and set the open ring box on the counter, then he turned one last, pointed glance toward her and headed for Jay's room.

16

Caroline crossed the kitchen and snatched the ring box Bobby left on the counter, staring into it as if she'd just found the Holy Grail. "Oh, baby!" She glanced up at Meagan and grinned. "So?"

Meagan sighed. What was she supposed to say? She didn't even completely understand how she felt about the situation. "So, what?"

Caroline grinned. "Never mind. I'll just be going now. You can call me tomorrow and let me know how it all turns out."

She nodded as her sister snapped the box shut, pressed it into her hand, and turned to go. "Caroline?"

Caroline turned, eyebrows raised, still wearing the same silly grin.

"Thanks."

"I guess it's been quite a night, huh?" With that she pulled the side door open and disappeared into the dusky evening light.

Meagan stepped to the door and watched as her sister backed out of the driveway and then drove down the street, the fading sound of the engine gradually superseded by the evening song of crickets, frogs, and cicadas. She closed her fingers around the small, velvet covered box in her hand as a slow smile took over. She hadn't even taken a close look at the ring. She ought to at least do that much before she gave him her answer.

Which would be what? Yes? No? Maybe?

Oh, who am I kidding? She hadn't even wanted to marry Kevin as much as she wanted Bobby. But did wanting it make it right? Would wanting it make it work? More than she wanted to marry Bobby, she *didn't* want another failed marriage. She didn't want to end up being fifty years old with two or three ex husbands, a grown child who resented her for not providing him a stable childhood, and all alone, anyway. She looked at the box and sudden curiosity twisted into tight knots in her stomach. Slowly she opened the lid.

She smiled despite herself. It was perfect.

The knots in her stomach vanished into a rush of warmth as she stared at the small square cut diamond set onto a thin gold band. Even in the dim overhead light of her kitchen the stone glittered and sparkled brilliantly, at least until tears blurred her vision and ruined the whole effect.

She snapped the box shut again and placed it back on the counter. She couldn't stand here agonizing over this now. They'd have to discuss it further after Jay was down. Bobby was really good with him, but that son of hers could easily sweet talk his way into story after story, until it was an hour past his bedtime. She'd better go make sure the task got completed.

She sniffed and wiped her tears away, then headed for Jay's bedroom. She stopped abruptly in the doorway, tears flowing back into her eyes as she absorbed the scene before her.

Bobby had Jay neatly tucked into his little bed which resided against the opposite wall, and was kneeling beside it with his back to her.

"Should we say your prayers now?"

A lump lodged itself in Meagan's throat at Bobby's softly spoken words. She leaned against the door casing, listening.

"Yeah."

She smiled at her son's soft whisper. For the past several months Jay had steadfastly refused to say his prayers, so she did it for him.

"OK, what do you usually pray about?"

Jay shrugged. "Mama prays."

"What does your Mama pray about?"

Jay shrugged again.

"Why don't I just go ahead and start?"

Jay nodded.

"OK." Bobby bowed his head. "Dear Lord, thank you for giving us this good day."

"Pizza." Jay whispered.

Bobby nodded. "Thank you for the pizza."

"Kevin." Jay whispered again.

There was a pause. Meagan tensed. But then Bobby continued. "And thank you for letting Kevin come for a visit."

Meagan pressed a hand to her mouth to stop a sob. She wasn't blind to Bobby's temper. But who could deny that he had it under such complete control. He'd come here to propose to her, only to find her ex husband having dinner with them. If he'd been all those things he thought he was he'd have flown into a rage over that, wouldn't he? How could he kneel there next to Jay's little bed, thanking God for her ex husband, and not realize what kind of man he was?

Her tears threatened to get noisy, so she stepped out of the room and leaned against the wall just outside Jay's door. Quietly as she could, she took a deep breath. Then she heard Bobby continue.

"And thank you, Lord, for giving Jay such a good Mama. Father, she loves him and takes such good care of him. And I pray that you'd let me take care of her. Help her to know that I love her, and that I'll always be around. And if it's not Your will that it works out between us, please take care of her and Jay. Keep them safe and happy."

There was a long pause then Jay whispered: "Rain."

"Oh, and Lord, please send us some rain. Is that all?" Bobby's deep quiet voice asked. Then, "OK. Thanks again, Lord. Amen."

"A-men." Jay's little voice echoed.

"OK, you go to sleep now."

"Can you come over again tomorrow?"

Bobby let out a weary sounding breath. "I sure hope so, Jay."

"You have to ask Mama?"

There was a short pause, then a brief, deep chuckle. "Yes. I have to ask your Mama."

"OK." She raised both hands and wiped the moisture from her face as she listened to the sound of Jay burrowing under his blanket and rolling over, getting comfortable. "Love you, Daddy."

Meagan almost gasped. The whole world stood still. She held her breath, waiting. From Jay's room, there came only silence. And more silence. She would swear her heart stopped beating. The silence stretched on for such a long moment that she wanted to poke her head into the room and make sure everything was all right. An instant before she acted on the impulse she heard Bobby draw a long, shaky breath and let it out again.

"I love you, too, Jay." Bobby's voice was thick and

hoarse.

Meagan breathed again as she listened to the sound of muffled footsteps on Jay's carpeted floor. They stopped, the light switch clicked. She caught her breath once more as Bobby stepped out the door, pulling it closed behind him.

She cast her gaze to the floor, fighting for composure. He stopped abruptly. Stood there silently. She wiped tears away with her finger tips and finally let the breath out, then raised her gaze to meet his. Whatever semblance of control she had managed to affect dissolved instantly.

Tears glimmered in his eyes, though none fell. He simply stood as if waiting for her to make the first move, to either run to him or throw him out for good.

"What do you...expect...me...to do?" Her voice was little more than a breathy whisper, and she had to pause to keep from choking on a sob. She pushed herself away from the wall and stalked into the living room. Another deep breath helped her get herself together. She turned back to find he'd followed right behind her. All the hurt and confusion of the past couple of weeks came pouring out. "You dump me. You tell me it's over for good between us. You give me a few weeks to actually adjust to the idea. Then you come back here, unannounced, telling me I'm your hope and your future. You ask me to marry you. Then you exchange 'I love you's' with my baby. And he...called you..." She felt her face contort in the wake of another wave of emotion. When she spoke again her voice was barely audible. "How do you expect me to react to that? Do you expect me to just throw myself into your arms?"

He expelled what sounded like a dying breath,

then he planted his hands on his hips and hung his head, shaking it almost desolately. Then he gave her a defeated little half shrug and looked back up at her. "Yeah." He nodded. "That's kind of how I hoped it would go."

She felt a tear fall and saw his expression soften. Then she felt a smile slowly begin to form, and watched as his expression mirrored it. Finally, she could contain the impulse no longer. She flung her arms around his neck and kissed him over and over. Instantly, his strong arms closed around her.

"Ah, Meagan," he said between kisses. "Don't you know how much I love you? Please believe me, baby. I won't leave you, and I'll never hurt you." He pulled her into a tighter embrace. When he spoke again the feel of his warm breath in her ear sent a shiver down her spine. "I never, in a thousand years, thought that I'd have the chance for a wife and a family. I didn't think I deserved it. I probably don't. But here it is, a gift from God. And what kind of idiot would I be if I let it slip right past me?"

"A pretty big one." She slid her hands up into his hair and cradled his head, pressing soft kisses to his face.

"I've been so miserable these past few weeks, thinking that it wasn't gonna work out between us. It's like I had a little sample of what life could be like, and then it all fell through. I thought I was gonna go crazy."

"You and me both." She murmured against his skin.

"But you gotta believe me, baby—"

"Bobby!"

He stopped short when she snapped his name.

"I believe you." She ran her gaze over every line and contour of his face, a deliberate smile working its way across her own face. "Now kiss me."

Also Available

Perfect Shelter, Book 1

"Curse God and die!"

That's the advice Job got from his wife, and it sounds good to Elaine Mallory. After a life spent seeking and doing God's will, the course of one turbulent spring strips her of everything but her life. Maybe she's not quite inclined to curse God and die, but she's got no problem turning from Him and running hard in the opposite direction.

Justin Barnet wants nothing more than to comfort Elaine and shelter her from more suffering. Her loss and departure leaves him devastated, and for years he waits for her return—years during which his own life falls apart. Now Elaine is back, and he has less to offer than ever.

As Elaine faces her grief for the first time since that tragic spring, will it reopen her heart to God's perfect shelter—and to Justin? Or will it drive her away again?

Return to Me, Book 2

Audrey Rhodes once walked the straight and narrow, but a terrible mistake changed the direction her life. Now former boyfriend and bad boy, Brent Thomason, is back in Blithe Settlement claiming newfound faith in God. Audrey's feelings for Brent haven't changed, but she has. Her life is in shambles. How can she be worthy of this new Brent's love?

Brent Thomason isn't proud of his past. Audrey had been his friend and his love, and he betrayed her. Now a veterinarian, he's returned home to work with Audrey's dad and make restitution for his misdeeds. Brent finds it's not so easy for people to accept his changed ways; still he must make things right with those he hurt, starting with Audrey.

As God directs their paths, Audrey discovers forgiveness is a two-edged sword...especially when she must first forgive herself. And Brent must accept God's will...even if it means losing Audrey a second time.

Thank you for purchasing this White Rose Publishing title. For other inspirational stories of romance, please visit our on-line bookstore at www.whiterosepublishing.com.

For questions or more information, contact us at titleadmin@whiterosepublishing.com.

White Rose Publishing
Where Faith is the Cornerstone of Love™
www.WhiteRosePublishing.com

May God's glory shine through
this inspirational work of fiction.

AMDG